PLAYING GOD

PLAYING GOD

by

Barbara Whitehead

Dales Large Print Books
Long Preston, North Yorkshire,
BD23 4ND, England.

British Library Cataloguing in Publication Data.

Whitehead, Barbara
    Playing God.

    A catalogue record of this book is
    available from the British Library

    ISBN   1-84262-457-1 pbk

First published in Great Britain in 1988 by Quartet Books Ltd.

Copyright © 1988 Barbara Whitehead

Cover illustration © Anthony Monaghan

The moral right of the author has been asserted

Published in Large Print 2006 by arrangement with
Barbara Whitehead

Dales Large Print is an imprint of Library Magna Books Ltd.

Printed and bound in Great Britain by
T.J. (International) Ltd., Cornwall, PL28 8RW

*This book is lovingly dedicated to my aunt
Muriel Kathleen Garner
whose delight in books, history,
and the Derbyshire countryside,
has always been an inspiration.*

The places in this book are real places, the plays are real plays. All the characters, however, are completely imaginary.

1

I am gracious and great, God without a
  beginning.
I am maker unmade, and all might is in me.
                                    The Barkers' Play

It was the last concert of the tour. The hall
was hot and full. Dark except where the
coloured lights probed across it, playing
with the blackness but always returning to
concentrate on the gyrating figure on the
stage. Sound rocked the auditorium, vibrating the walls, drowning the screams of the
girls. Poison Peters was working up to a
crescendo to beat the crescendo his whole
performance had been. They saw him in the
flesh, yet through their memories of his
videos, his record sleeves, his TV appearances. At last it ended. He left the stage.
They let him go slowly, as though they
would drag the flesh from his bones.

In a quiet road in the ancient city of York,
Tom Churchyard had parked his bicycle.
Sydney Absolom came by at that moment
and together they walked past the pale stone
walls of the city towards Monk Bar.

'There'll be the devil to pay over this,' said Absolom.

He was an oldish man with hair which seemed to have settled on his head like a small inconsequent cloud. He looked very like the painting of a saint on the fourteenth-century glass of the window of the north choir aisle of All Saints Church. They were going to a meeting of the Medieval Reconstruction Society (known as MRS) in an old stone cell of a room slung high over one of the busy streets which led into the heart of the congested town.

'I can't believe it. They wouldn't choose *him* as Christ,' replied Thomas.

They arrived at the meeting; the speaker was already there; nothing more was said between them until afterwards, when the time arrived for coffee and biscuits.

'There'll be the devil to pay over this,' said Mr Absolom again.

'What's the matter?' asked Julia Bransby, who had been giving them a lecture on early woven fabrics. She had turned to Thomas Churchyard, the chairman, beside her.

'You haven't heard? It was in the Press. I can hardly believe it myself.'

'I've only just got back from Manchester. I haven't even been home. Adam had to get his own tea.'

'Bruce Exelby has named his Christ.'

'At last! You've been rehearsing for weeks,

haven't you? What's taken him so long? There's only one professional actor in the cast, you wouldn't think he would leave the choice until the last minute like this.'

'They stir up a lot of publicity about it these days. It all helps to remind people that we have a festival, that they can see a performance of medieval drama without going to Oberammergau, that each time there is this search for the Christ.'

'Well, and who's he ended up with?'

'You won't guess.' Thomas Churchyard took a mouthful of his powdered coffee and hot water in its expanded polystyrene beaker. He seemed reluctant to tell her. Then at last he said, 'He's chosen Poison Peters.'

'Poison Peters? You've got to be joking.'

'No, unfortunately.'

'Not Poison Peters that ghastly pop singer?'

'Afraid so.'

'Not to play Christ in the mystery plays?'

'Yes.'

Now the name was actually spoken among them, the enormity of the producer's action seemed to grow and glower in the still air of that medieval room, poised over the thoroughfare, held in quietness over the busy cars and people.

'Well!' Julia drank her coffee, unable to say anything else. Absolom looked at them, went over to his raincoat (he was never without it, even in May), pulled a newspaper out of the pocket and came over. He had been listening to their conversation. 'POISON CAST AS CHRIST' screamed the headline, and below it was a large photograph of the pop star looking as though he was about to take a bite out of a microphone, face distorted and deathly pale, hair in a sort of aureole of blond spikes.

Absolom looked heavily at Julia, and repeated his words.

'There'll be the devil to pay over this.'

'I should just think there will! The whole city will be up in arms. It's a desecration. What a person to choose. Drugs, orgies, smashing up hotel rooms, you name it...'

They all remembered the reports of occasions when Poison had been disgracefully sick in public; the damage done by his band; the hotel carpets ruined; the trans-dressing, being refused entry to a prudish Catholic country because he was dressed as a woman; the stark white make-up in the daytime; the hair in a variety of fluorescent colours; the groupies thrown out by hotel managements...

'There is a feeling of outrage through the city. You'll see. There'll be letters in the Press about it tomorrow. More than that,' said Absolom darkly. 'There'll be *something done*. It won't be allowed to go through. There'll be a stop put to it.'

'I should think there might well,' replied Thomas.

'It's an insult. What does he think he's doing? It's shaming that such a man should be given the role of Christ. Man? He doesn't deserve the name of *man* – filthy creature.'

'It is a surprise, certainly.'

'A surprise?'

'A shock, if you like.'

Sydney Absolom's face was flushed under the small round-edged cloud of hair.

'I think it's disgusting,' added the secretary, Sally Vause, a plump, lively woman, catching hold of the plate of biscuits as though she was fielding a cricket ball.

'I'd better go.' Julia put down her beaker. 'Thanks.'

'We'd like you to accept a small token of our gratitude,' said the treasurer, Velvet Smith, coming up with a white envelope.

'You shouldn't have,' said Julia. 'I didn't expect anything. You're such a small society. I'm sure you're short of funds.'

'Yes. But not so short that we can't acknowledge an excellent lecture like yours, Mrs Bransby.'

The pleasantries went on.

Julia had not lived in the city very long, but as she looked round the room she found she knew, at least vaguely, most of the people in it. Apart from herself there were eleven – four men and seven women.

15

The chairman, Thomas Churchyard, struck her as one of those big dependable men who were nice to have around. Sydney Absolom was so earnest about everything that he could be amusing. George Grindal, a dear old man, she had met when she had been called in to advise on a textile in the Minster. Then there was a roly-poly couple, Mr and Mrs Moore, who were always together like Tweedledum and Tweedledee. The women she knew less well. The secretary had arranged the talk; she was the retired head of an office department. Velvet Smith, about forty, did the society's typing and looked as though she worked in an office. The newsletter editor was a rather aristocratic type of middle-aged housewife who probably had not worked for money since her marriage. Then there was a university student, rather quiet and mousy. The other two were friends in their thirties whom Julia seemed to see wherever she went, difficult to place, slightly arty. In fact Betty and Sandra Tweddle ran a flower shop together and were cousins.

Thomas smiled in the direction of Velvet Smith a little apologetically. She was an insignificant person and when she was not in his line of vision he always forgot her. So he made up for it with his smile. Then he took both his beaker and Julia's over to where the secretary and newsletter editor were beginning to tidy up in the corner.

The society had its meetings in different places throughout the city, as varied as possible. This room had been loaned them for one night only by the Boy Scouts. It was in one of the barrier entrances to the city, and the stir of traffic could hardly be heard through the thick chilly stone walls; really an ideal place for a meeting of the MRS.

Somehow the women members had managed to bring up a supply of water and a camping Gaz stove, and refreshments had appeared as usual. Now they were rinsing things in a bucket which was later to be carried down the steep, narrow stone stairs into the street.

You couldn't find anything more ersatz and modern than the coffee they'd drunk, Thomas thought, not for the first time; home-brewed ale out of horn beakers would be more authentic and not as much trouble.

If only this wretched news had not come to spoil a very pleasant evening.

'I'll see you out,' Thomas said to Julia as she put on her coat.

'There's no need, really.'

'We're all going, anyway. At present we see one another so often there's no need for our usual business discussion.'

'You're all in the mystery plays, I suppose?'

'We're all involved, one way or another.

What would you expect of a medieval reconstruction society?'

'Of course.'

They went down the stairs. Outside, the tender dusk of late spring was gathering.

'I'm on my moped, actually,' Julia Bransby said. 'It's parked across the road.'

'Cheers, then.' Thomas Churchyard nodded. He watched her slim figure in a neat grey coat vanish. He went for his bicycle. It was always good to see that it was still there. No wonder the city had a road called Thief Lane and one called Bad Bargain – no bicycle was safe. And it was a relief to get away from the explosive feeling which had arisen when Sydney Absolom had raised the matter of the Christ. Here out in the street Thomas breathed deeply. He liked Julia Bransby, and wondered vaguely when he would see her again. They did meet from time to time. In a city like York people with similar interests could not help bumping into one another, for all the different societies were like the interlocking Olympic circles. The Georgians, the Philosophical, the YA-YAS, the MRS, the Victorians, the Dickens Society, the Thirties, the Family History, the After Eights, you name it...

Looking not like a pea on a drum but like a drum on a pea, Churchyard mounted his bicycle. He was a big man and bulky, with a large head and impressive though scarcely

18

handsome features, and riding he gave something of the impression of a circus elephant balancing on a ball – the combination of size and dainty precision. Silent and non-polluting, he slid into the stream of vehicles and became part of it.

Goodramgate was narrow and turned at angles which made it impossible to see ahead. The bright mixture of cars jerked forward, played follow-my-leader round a parked van, moved slowly past the colossal side of the Minster, was held up by a stream of pedestrians at the zebra crossing. Churchyard could move more freely than most. He travelled steadily up the gutter, looking round, glancing at shop windows where some lights were now burning, admiring the pretty girl tourists in their summer clothes, noticing how the soft dusk caressed the bronze-green of the Henry Moore statue in its grove of trees at the east end of the Minster, lifting his eyes for a split second to the darkness of the Minster itself. Soon surely they would be turning on the floodlights, so that it could be seen clearly again, unshadowed, creamy and proud over the city.

A sudden gust of dry dusty air caught him as he passed St Michael le Belfrey. Ahead there was a dapple of colour as a group of American tourists crossed the road. Churchyard moved steadily past the gables of the Dean Court Hotel – once a row of prebends'

houses – to the traffic lights and the screaming bed of shocking pink geraniums – turned
right – moved into the left lane past the
twinkle of gilt on the black ironwork of the
Georgian crescent of St Leonard's – went
with the green filter light into Bootham –
passed Alexa's Tasty Nibbles Sandwich Bar
in its Tudor-looking frontage – and, leaving
the core of the ancient city behind him,
moved out into the suburbs.

A few minutes later he turned left into a
road which had been built across the centre
of the grounds of what had once been a
gentleman's residence. Now it was a modern
small estate. Ahead he could see a removal
van; his new neighbours must have arrived.

As Thomas spun silently down the road
towards the Harrogate van, he saw that the
moving-in process was nearly complete. The
men were handing back tea mugs to a slim
young woman and climbing into their cab.
As he reached the van its engine started.

Turning into his own drive Thomas felt a
twinge of conscience. OK, it was late – after
nine o'clock. But he felt he ought to give the
newcomers a word of welcome. There
wouldn't be time in the morning, and it was
the kind of thing the sooner done the better.
He put the bicycle into the garage beside his
car, locked up, and wandered back indecis-
ively to the front of the house.

The houses had been built around 1960,

and were semi-detached. He had become used to living on the other side of the wall to an old couple, and now he could see it was all going to be different. An upstairs light was on and he could hear sounds of children preparing for bed. The young woman had vanished. Then he saw her through the uncurtained window of the children's room.

'She won't want me butting in at present,' he thought, and went back again, into the garden at the rear. Here it was different. There was no light from the house, but a dim glow from a newly-lit pipe, and the scent of Holland House, told him that one at least of his new neighbours was available. Thomas moved towards the irregular line of shrubs and small trees which hid the posts and wire separating the two gardens.

'Evening,' said his new neighbour, taking the pipe from his mouth. 'Robert Southwell.' And, coming close to a gap in the shrubs, he extended a hand dimly seen in the gathering darkness.

'Thomas Churchyard,' – taking the hand.

'Bob,' amended Robert Southwell.

'And Tom, of course. Welcome to York and to Ouse Avenue.'

'We've come from Harrogate.'

'I noticed Harrogate on the van.'

'We think we're lucky to have got a move to York. We're looking forward to living here.'

21

'Can I offer you and your wife coffee – can I help at all?'

'Linda's got it all under control.'

In a few minutes Bob discovered that Tom was a bachelor (and Tom, remembering Julia Bransby, wondered why he was). Tom found out that the Southwells' two children were called Susan and Paul.

'Have you come to join a York company?' Tom felt he was making the inquiry about as delicately as a bull in a china shop but it helped to get the basic facts about people straight at the outset, then you knew where you were with them.

'Not exactly. I'm CID – Detective Chief Inspector. Transferred to York on promotion.'

'I'm British Telecom myself. Engineering. I should have thought we were a pretty quiet place from your point of view,' said Thomas.

'Oh, I don't know. The city seems to be crowded with people at the moment, many of them foreigners. I might uncover the odd international diamond-smuggling ring or two,' said Bob.

After a slight pause, Tom said, 'You'll find there are several different cities in one. There's the tourists' York; the one you know already, the one everybody sees before they come to live here. Then there's the incomers' York; that's the one you and I belong to. Most of the societies in the city are full of ex-pats.'

Thomas had been thinking about this as he rode home. He went on. 'Then there's the native York; people who were born here of York families; you don't get many of them in the societies. Their view of the place is quite different. Most of the time they aren't interested in the antiquities and think it would be just as useful if the Minster were pulled down to make more parking space. They see a side of the place I never see at all. It is as if separate worlds exist in parallel. They can't see mine and I can't see theirs, yet we're physically in the same place living and working together.'

'You're very involved in local voluntary activities, then?' asked Bob.

'I suppose I am ... I've just come back from a meeting of the one I'm chairman of and I've been thinking how odd it is that we only have three members who were born in York.'

'Linda's very interested in the mystery plays,' said Bob. 'She's thrilled to bits because we'll be able to go for once.'

'Now that's something quite a lot of the real Yorkists are involved in, as well as ex-pats.'

'Are *you*?'

'Oh, yes. In fact I'm acting this year.'

Summing him up through the gathering darkness Bob said, 'You don't look the type.'

'I'm playing God,' Tom replied in suitably

modest tones.

'You don't mean to tell me we've come to live next door to God?'

'Well, yes.'

'I can see you in that part. Large and impressive. And your voice fits.'

'Thank you for those few kind words.'

'Good Lord!' Bob drew in his breath. Tom looked at him sharply. Bob was not making uncalled-for-jokes. Thomas could see that the pale egg-shape of his face had become a half-moon profile with inquiring nose. Turning to look in the same direction Thomas saw that the Minster floodlighting had been turned on, and the great building hung suspended against the night sky like a vision.

'Yes ... I suppose I've got used to it ... even blasé about living where it can be seen like this...'

'How could anyone ever become blasé about something like that?' asked Bob.

'Wait five years.'

'If I waited fifty I could never get over it.'

They stood in silence for a while, and Bob let his pipe go out. Linda came out of the house to join them, and her perfume replaced the smell of Holland House. At last she broke the spell by inviting Thomas to come in for a coffee.

'I came into the garden with the intention of asking you the same thing.'

'All right then,' said Bob, 'we will. But

only for half an hour. The kids are asleep in a strange place, and we're pretty ready for bed ourselves.'

'You can step across the wire near the house.'

Bob and Linda looked around them with interest. The house was a duplicate of their own. The small hall had three doors and the stairway opening off it and a cupboard for coats, so there was virtually no wall-space; a smallish mirror framed with dull carved gilt hung on the only bit of wall; they stood on a thick plain carpet of welcoming crimson. They followed Thomas into his kitchen and perched on a couple of stout ash stools. In a few minutes he had a percolator bubbling on the stove. The floor was crimson linoleum which exactly matched the colour of the hall carpet.

'Lived here long?' asked Linda.

'Five years. I took over the carpets, curtains and decorations from the previous owners.' He had noticed her look around. 'Afraid I'm always too busy to get round to altering things.'

'I like it the way it is. Tell me something about the mystery plays,' said Linda. 'I love anything from the Middle Ages. It's really my favourite period.'

'Oh, yes.' At first Thomas looked at her blankly, as if he didn't know where to start. 'Well, they were suppressed in 1572 and not performed again until 1951.'

'And then they became an annual event?'

'Not annual. Every three years or so. There's a lot of work involved.' He found a leaflet on the shelf and handed it to her.

'"The plays performed by the craft guilds of the city,"' read Linda. 'Were they like trade unions?'

'More or less.'

'On the Feast of Corpus Cristi which falls in May or June...'

'The Body of Christ.'

'The Feast of the Body of Christ!' repeated Bob. 'Sounds rather gruesome.'

'The Middle Ages often were,' Thomas turned to him seriously. 'Think of the plague. Think of the charnel houses. Gruesomeness was definitely part of their lives much more than it is of ours, don't you think so?'

'I hadn't thought about it,' replied Bob.

Linda was still looking at the leaflet. 'Originally forty-eight plays! They must have taken a while to get through!'

'All day, dawn to dusk. They show first God and heaven, then the fall of Lucifer and the angels, the creation of man (and woman of course),' he added hastily to Linda. 'All that part shows the need for man's redemption. Then the story of the life of Christ, the redeemer, from the birth right through to the resurrection and ascension. The epilogue shows the end of the world.'

'Gosh,' said Bob comprehensively.

'The forty-eight plays have been amalgamated so that they flow together into one long one.'

'I should hope so.'

Thomas turned round with the mugs of coffee. He was glad to have the chance to study his new neighbours in the light. Linda was dark-haired, young, pleasant-looking, dressed in pale grey and remarkably clean-looking when you remembered that they'd been moving house all day. Bob was tall – nearly as tall as Thomas – and reminded him of Fred Astaire with glasses. He looked bright, alert, perceptive, even though he was perched, temporarily at rest, on the ash stool.

'Just reading that booklet can't give you any idea of what a performance is like – the drama, beauty and majesty of the whole thing – the way the audience and cast are all bound up together in seeing the great story through...' Thomas produced a plate of garibaldi biscuits. 'I hope you like these.'

'I do,' said Linda, taking three.

'In 1951 the whole thing was done with great reverence, as a religious experience. You can see how things have changed.'

'Yes. Loads of adverts. Potted biographies. The plays themselves take rather a back seat.'

'It was inevitable I suppose when they became a tourist attraction. But there's a furore in the town tonight.'

'What about?' A look of keenness crossed Bob's face.

'We always have a professional director nowadays, and a professional actor as Christ. It's become something of an excitement every time to see who the director chooses as his Christ. This time Bruce Exelby is directing – have you heard of him? He works a lot in London – and he's chosen Poison Peters.'

'I can't believe it,' said Linda.

'Neither can anyone.'

'It's sacrilege!'

'That's what the city thinks. There is fury over it.'

'But his whole life-style...'

'It's nothing but a publicity gimmick. The decision has been spun out until the last possible moment – we've been rehearsing weeks and there's only a fortnight to go before production. When Peters arrives he'll be lucky if he isn't greeted with rotten eggs or something worse.'

'We'll have to provide a police escort,' smiled Bob.

'I expect you'd do that anyway. He had one when he gave a pop concert at the university. That was nearly a riot. Thousands of pounds' worth of damage.'

'Is his career slipping a bit? Whatever could make him accept the part of Christ? He's not an actor.'

'I don't know.'

'Bob, you'll be here all night.' Linda got up. 'Early start in the morning. Good of you to ask us round, Tom. I'm thrilled to bits about the mystery plays. You'll have to meet the children tomorrow. I'll be telling them all about it.'

'Anything you want to know? The dustmen collect on Fridays and two milkmen deliver down this road. Northern Dairies at seven o'clock and the Co-op a bit later.'

'What time is the post?' asked Bob.

'About eight.'

'Thanks for the welcome. It's taken our minds off the traumas of the day. We're really looking forward to living here.'

'Great to have you as neighbours.'

Linda lightly clasped Thomas's outstretched hand. 'Thanks for the coffee and the garibaldi biscuits.'

Left alone, Thomas felt pleased. He hoped he hadn't bored them about the mystery plays, but they had seemed interested … and the plays filled his own life just now.

If they were going to live in York they would have to get used to the fact that the past might be dead but it wouldn't lie down – it was all around and among present-day living, giving it a dimension in time. He felt it was an enrichment, and couldn't imagine how people could live in new towns, where there was no ancient heart still beating.

2

Hail, doomsman dread that all shall doom!
Hail, that all quick and dead shall lout!
Hail, whom worship shall most beseem!
Hail, whom all things shall dread and
  doubt!
  We welcome thee
  Hail and welcome, of all about
  To our city!

The Skynners' Play

The first outrage over the appointment of
Poison Peters had hardly died down before
a second wave began, because having
accepted the role he seemed in no hurry to
play it.

The director, Bruce Exelby, had arrived.
He had been to the city several times since
his appointment the previous September.
He always left York shaking as though it had
been visited by a whirlwind, and the work he
organized other people to do kept them
fully occupied until his next descent.

In January the casting for the major amateur parts had been carried out, in February
the crowds had been cast. There was the

31

perennial shortage of men coming forward to act. The male sex was happier fiddling with the scenery or fixing wires for the lighting, or passing its opinion on the design of the set.

On Shakespeare's birthday, rehearsals had begun. The flying visits of Bruce Exelby became more frequent. Christ had been named in late May, the three weeks of performances were to begin in the first week of June. Exelby took up residence in the flat on the top floor of St Mary's Lodge, and moved into the last two weeks of rehearsal, where the crowd joined the principals of the cast.

It was as well that police crowd control had been provided for Poison Peters when at long last he arrived at York station. Sergeant Smith and a couple of constables were in readiness. A large crowd began to gather. There were Poison Peters's ardent fans, mostly dressed in black but with multicoloured hair, like a carnival of crows. The media were there in force; the ITV unit was over from Leeds, with brilliant lights and a loud-hailer blaring; Radio York was there with a van and microphone; the reporters from the *York Evening Press* and the *Yorkshire Post* both had their notebooks and attendant photographers. Even the national dailies were interested. A freelance journalist was there with a commission from several of them for a report if there was anything worth reporting.

Bruce Exelby had insisted on the leading members of the cast going down with him to meet the pop star, so Thomas Churchyard had had to ask for time off work.

'You realise you're going to be away for three full weeks for this damn pantomime of yours,' said the executive engineer heavily.

'Yes.'

'That takes every shred of what's left of your leave for the rest of this leave year, Tom. It'll be no use you saying you want any more time off.'

'*I* don't want to go to meet the wretched man. It looks as if I'm condoning his appointment, and I don't, none of those involved in the plays do.'

'You don't?'

'No, I don't,' repeated Tom heatedly. 'He's quite unsuitable. This sort of thing brings into disrepute a fine and precious part of our heritage. Something that means a lot to me personally. When the committee appoint a director they give him a free hand; that's fair enough; how else could he operate? And you've got to trust him. OK, so this time Bruce Exelby's gone and done this. It's only fair to say that otherwise he's good; the whole production's shaping up well. It's really developing a terrific feeling. That's why it's so sad this is happening. But we've just got to weather it and make the best we can of it. It's no use Sydney Absolom and the rest kicking up a stink. They may as well grin and bear it.'

'So you're going to grin and bear it at the station at eleven o'clock, are you? What, in costume? Have you got your nightie with you?'

'If you let me have the time off. And no, I'm going as I am.'

'Go on, then. Don't be away longer than you have to. I'll see if I can put it down as a public relations exercise. If the press are there make sure they know that you're there by kind courtesy of British Telecom.'

In the end, the police had to put a cordon across the narrow part of the entrance to the station. 'I need help to deal with this lot,' Sergeant Smith had radioed to his station. 'There's crowds arriving with banners...'

A group of constables came in support, and the duty inspector arrived to take overall control.

Thomas stood waiting near the barrier as part of a line-up which included the Lord Mayor (wearing his chain of office), the Lady Mayoress, the Sheriff (wearing his chain of office) and the Sheriff's Lady; Clare Black, a prefect at Queen Elizabeth's School, who was playing the Virgin Mary; James Bowes, who was Lucifer – a large and important part with a real opportunity for character acting – and Humphrey Hale, a local solicitor, who was the Archangel Gabriel.

Bruce Exelby arrived. He was dressed up for the occasion, in a black soft leather bomber jacket over a fawn shirt and cream jumper, and fawn cord casual trousers. Giving Clare, the Virgin, a charming smile, he lounged over to her.

'Big chance coming up,' he said caressingly. 'Next stop RADA and then the West End, name in lights!'

'You're teasing me, Mr Exelby.' Clare dropped her eyelashes and blushed.

'Not me, I'm renowned for my talent spotting.' His voice dropped and, lips close to her ear, he murmured something more. Thomas could not hear him, but could see the effect on Clare. He felt irritated; the director often irritated him. Why did Exelby have to go turning the girl's head? She was a good actress, of course, but she was a good all-rounder and Thomas happened to know that she had done exceptionally well in her O levels and, like her boyfriend the Youngest Shepherd, was hoping to go to Cambridge. The career of an actress was glamorous but it could also be a worrying one, largely spent 'resting'. Weren't women scientists and engineers and statesmen (he hesitated to include politicians) just as useful?

He had plenty of time to think of these things, for the train was late.

The police could not stop the missiles

which hurtled through the air at the waiting group. Two squashy tomatoes found their mark, one among the elaborately-worked links of the mayoral chain and the other in the hat of the Sheriff's Lady. Thomas fidgeted, glowered at the noisy crowd, and was sure he glimpsed some familiar faces, including that of Sydney Absolom.

At last the train pulled into the vibrating station. After the tomato-throwing the police had cleared the crowd from the area of the ivory-coloured terrazzo tiles of the entrance back to the grey drab flooring of pavement and covered roadway. The only people allowed through were *bona fide* travellers who passed the line-up of notables with a furtive and apologetic air. Bruce Exelby had gone onto the platform and soon could be seen walking over the bridge talking animatedly to two other men; one undistinguished, slightly above middle height, weighed down with suitcases; the other was undoubtedly Poison Peters. A porter followed behind with a loaded trolly.

Those who had only seen Poison on the television and video might have been surprised how small and slim he was; five foot five in his socks; even with built-up heels he was barely five seven. His tight trousers and built-up jacket were of silver lamé, and worn over a sweat shirt of black fabric as light-absorbing as velvet, embroidered across the chest with a broad silver star. But after the first glance no one noticed his clothes. It was that dead-white face with its rouged lips, the great aureole of spikes of hair bleached until it was almost white, the busy gesturing hands, which riveted attention.

Catching sight of the media persons Poison carried out what Thomas could only call a cavort. He leapt into the air, punching high with his right fist, mouth wide open in a Comanche yell. Flash bulbs spurted light from the cameras of the waiting media men. One of them caught the shot which, blown up and used a thousand times over, was to become the symbol of the year's mystery plays – Poison, against the dark shadows of the background in which you could just pick out Bruce Exelby, the road manager and the porter, exploding in energy and light, for he had leaped into a shaft of sun and looked in the photograph as though he was ten feet above the ground, more demonic than Christ-like.

Tom thought of the ordinary people of the city, thought of Sydney Absolom, shut his eyes and shuddered. Outside, the teenage fans in the crowd set up a wail that sounded like the cry of lost souls.

There were at least three groups from the university. There were students among the fans; then there was the group from the students' Christian Union who had a large red banner proclaiming 'WE WILL NOT HAVE A DEVIL TO PLAY CHRIST,' and a third group containing several lecturers under a board on a pole proclaiming 'FREE SPEECH AND FREE DRAMA'; no one was quite sure what they stood for. Another section of the crowd was from the Church and had a large proportion of dog collars. They were making a dignified silent protest and Sergeant Black had no need to worry about them. Their placard, neatly lettered, read 'WHAT THINK YE OF CHRIST? Matt. 22.42.' There was also a noisy group of fundamentalists. They began to shout 'Out with Poison!' and unrolled their banner which said 'NO BLASPHEMY', while other parts of the crowd had placards reading, 'GO HOME PETERS,' and 'KEEP YORK CLEAN – BAN POISON.'

After that much photographed leap into the air Poison Peters had walked down the remaining steps, through the barrier, and up to the line of the reception quite calmly and in an ordinary way. In a minute Thomas found his hand being shaken, and looked down into a pair of heavily mascara-ed golden brown eyes.

'We'll get to know one another real well, I expect,' said Poison.

'I'm sure,' said Tom. 'Not too well, I hope,' he added hastily to himself. His hand tingled from the quick bony grip. In a few seconds Poison moved on to greet the next in line; seconds later he passed through the foyer with the official party quickly bunching together at his heels.

As he appeared there was a scuffle as the police pounced on someone in the crowd and confiscated a quantity of rotten tomatoes. The fans screamed and sobbed for joy. Poison grabbed a sparkling guitar from his road manager, posed with it held across his loins, and then held it in the air as he stretched out his arms to his fans as if to embrace them.

A tomato missed him and took the mayoral Rolls Royce full in the bumper. An egg dashed itself to pieces at his feet. The TV cameras rolled. The man from Radio York advanced with his microphone. The reporters broke into a volley of questions.

'Have you ever acted in a play before, Mr Peters?'

'There's no other play like this one, yeah?'

'Do you know that there is opposition in the city to your playing the part of Christ?'

'I have been chosen, yeah?'

A tomato sliced itself on the strings of his guitar.

'Have you ever been to York before?'

'This is like my first trip to your beautiful city, yeah?'

'We'll have a press conference in the Mansion House,' interposed the Lord Mayor.

The car doors swung open. With a last open-armed gesture to his fans, Poison bent and manoeuvred his head into the long black limo without damaging a single spike of hair. The civic party hastily climbed into the official cars, made sure the windows were wound up, and sat back with sighs of relief.

Poison kept up an interplay with his fans through his closed window. The sleek cars, now well spattered with tomatoes, glided slowly away from the station, the city's arms on a tiny flag fluttering from the nose of the first.

'I'll get back to work,' said Tom Churchyard with an air of relief.

'You won't,' replied Bruce Exelby. 'There's a civic reception and lunch at the Mansion House. Get in.' The assistant director had brought Exelby's Porsche up, next in line.

Tom found the civic lunch an agony. Fortunately he was not near Poison, except for one moment when they were jostled close in the crowd as trays of drinks were passed round.

'Got my own, yeah?' said Poison, bringing out a vodka bottle from his pocket and taking a noisy swig. 'I don't drink any sort of rubbish.'

Tom was grateful that it was a buffet lunch. He grabbed a few shrimp vol-au-vents and decided he could sustain himself until the tea-trolley came round in the afternoon at work. He would just have time to pop into St Olave's parish room, where the wardrobe people were working, and have the last-minute fitting he had promised Sally Vause.

'He'll barely have time to learn his lines,' said Sally, secretary of MRS, and wardrobe mistress to the plays. 'Have you seen this?' She flapped a tabloid newspaper in Tom's face and it fell open at a montage of images of Poison Peters. Spiky eyelashes, bleached white hair, pale face, great lips open wide in a spongy mouthing of sound. 'He must finish these concerts exhausted, then go to bed with half a dozen groupies.'

'Not if he's that exhausted.'

'Well! He'll be high on adrenalin if not heroin or coke – probably runs through a few groupies instead of taking sleeping pills. How's he going to find time to learn to give full quality to medieval verse?'

'He'll be here full time. We all have to fit it in round normal work.'

'Humph,' said Sally. Her needle made vicious darts at the cloth of Tom's costume, short stabbing movements leaving a trail of thread. Tom flinched and looked at the ceiling and thought of England.

Julia Bransby entered the parish hall.

'How's it going?'

'Very well, really,' answered Sally.

41

'Everything's looking super. Where's Velvet?'

'Oh, she's around somewhere. No, she's gone.'

Tom didn't like standing there like a dressmaker's lay figure and not being spoken to.

'She's such a self-effacing person,' he put in. 'One doesn't always notice her.'

'I don't think she's really self-effacing,' answered Julia. 'I think there's something very strange and deep in her, she makes me feel she is waiting for someone or something...'

'Oh, Julia!' exclaimed Sally Vause. 'How you love dramatizing people! Even dull predictable women like Velvet. All she's waiting for is the next bus.'

They dissolved into laughter.

'I'm ravenous,' said Tom. 'All I've had for lunch is three shrimp vol-au-vents. Would you like to join me for a sandwich and a beer, Julia? There's a pub in Marygate.' Work can wait, he thought.

'I'd like that.'

It was the first time Poison Peters had seen the place where the mystery plays were to be performed. He was part of the informal procession walking the short distance from the Mansion House, along Lendal, across busy Museum Street and in through the gates of the Museum Gardens. The crowds had mostly grown tired of waiting outside the Mansion House for the civic lunch to be over. Anyway, lunch hour was up and many of them, even on flexitime, had had to go back to work. The streets were full, but with summer tourists who were not really aware of Poison's presence in the city, or of its significance.

Once in the Gardens the group with Poison at their centre moved in a phalanx through the undulating, sloping, glancing landscape; the great trees made grateful with their summer shade the parched grass; men in shirtsleeves and girls with bare midriffs lay around, some eating, some studying guide books about York.

Ahead was the unlovely back of a stand of seats; the area was partitioned off; a few of the people concerned with the plays were around.

It was not until Poison had been admitted through the barrier and had passed through the grandstand, that he could take in the ruins of St Mary's Abbey, in front of and around which the set had been built. The row of stone arches rose against a warm blue sky, lovely, serene, and breathtaking. In front of them and up to them lay the centre stage, but there were slopes, and steps, and holes through which one could see other things.

Poison had just finished a gruelling concert tour. His thin body was taut with nervous energy, his face expressionless.

'Show me my pad, yeah?' he said to Bruce Exelby. Turning to those of the civic party who had come to the Museum Gardens with him he said, 'Be seeing ya, right?' He raised his hand in farewell.

With director and road manager he walked round the end of the ruins.

'You're not suggesting he sleeps in a graveyard?' The road manager was aghast.

'The caravan's right here.'

It was. Tucked away round the end of the set, next to but not in the graveyard, in a quiet spot near a bowling green, was the silver-grey caravan with its wide bright silver streak along the side.

'Right,' said Poison.

'You're sleeping in my flat,' Exelby said to the road manager. 'You did want to be isolated, Poison, isn't that right?'

'Yeah. Where I can do my own thing.'

'Here's the key of the set. It's all locked when we aren't here. You're inside the enclosure, quite private. The whole gardens are locked up at night of course – we'll have to see about access for you. You can probably have the spare key to the gates on to Marygate. I use that entrance to reach my flat.'

'Right,' said Poison.

Bruce Exelby's head was full of images of what might happen at night in the caravan. 'What do you want to do for the rest of the

44

day?' he asked. 'I'd suggest you do a bit of sightseeing but if the antis catch sight of you you would get mobbed.'

'I'll disguise myself, right?'

The thin garish figure went into the caravan. The key clicked in the lock. The blinds went down.

Later in the day, after work, Thomas Churchyard went back to St Olave's parish room. He walked through the Museum Gardens and out through the Marygate entrance, then down Almery Lane.

Ahead of him a group of Devils in scarlet and black burst out of the room door, and came screaming and tumbling down the lane. They wore masks like the sanctuary knocker of Durham Cathedral – great beaky frightening things of papier-mâché, with horns; they carried forks, or tridents; an old lady ahead of Thomas shrank against the wall in fright.

'Behave yourselves, lads!' cried Tom, but was only answered by waving tridents and hands waggling defiantly at ears.

'You wouldn't think they're nicely brought up lads from a public school,' said Tom to the old lady, who looked as if she might never recover.

'Oh. Are they the seven boys from St Giles? I heard about them on Radio York.'

'You know what they're like at that age.'

45

'Oh yes.' The old lady looked brighter. 'I've had boys myself, you know.'

Thomas nodded at her and went into the dusty, crowded parish room.

'I see the little Devils are ready.'

'Little Devils is right. Velvet, fetch that costume for God.'

Thomas looked at Velvet with more interest than usual as she helped him on with the costume. She had some redeeming features, after all. Her teeth were very good, he noticed when she smiled at him. He shook out the folds of fabric.

'That's much better.'

'Do you think it's quite full enough?' came a strong penetrating voice; Tom knew without turning that it was Jane Bugg, thankfully not one of MRS, but very much one of the mystery-play scene.

'Quite full enough, thank you, Jane,' said Sally Vause, with exaggerated patience.

'The medieval cloak was cut on a full circle,' went on Jane, 'hence the flowing folds. Julia Bransby would tell you.'

'She already has, thank you very much.'

'As I was saying to *Bruce*–' went on Jane.

As if on cue Bruce Exelby swaggered into the room. Since the reception he had changed back into his more normal clothing. Although he must be, Tom thought, about forty, Exelby still wore the kind of things he had worn for the last twenty-five years –

today it was his usual, a checked lumberjack shirt and faded jeans. He combed his curly black hair carefully forward and his shoes were handmade, his huge metal wristwatch gold. Otherwise the years had changed him little, only adding a stone to his weight, rounding out all his contours.

'How's it going?'

'I think the cloak should be *fuller,* don't you, dear *Bruce?*' asked Jane Bugg. Sally Vause cut in with, 'All this re-dying and making new costumes has meant a lot of work.'

'You've got the effect I wanted. Subtlety. Harmonies of colour are important to me. I speak to the audience not only through groupings and disposition of actors but through the audience's subconscious appreciation of the colours I use.'

Thomas looked around hastily to see what gallery Exelby was playing to, apart from Jane Bugg who was looking adoring and gathering up his every syllable. Nearly everyone had stopped to listen and there were at least a dozen figures in the room, busy among the host of garments in colours from white to black, brilliant yellow to russet and deep brown, pale to deepest blue, with flashes of scarlet and purple.

'These vegetable dyes took no end of researching,' grumbled Sally. 'They are messy and time-consuming and will fade. The Burco boiler is practically worn out and so is the spin-dryer. If it hadn't been for Julia Bransby's advice and research I don't know how we'd have done it.'

Exelby did not care how people did things as long as they were done.

'The quality is incomparable.'

Thomas felt bound to agree. The colours were a triumph. They had the curious quality of not clashing; of looking rich and varied and yet all of a piece. Exelby turned to Jane Bugg.

'And how is my Porteress today?' he asked, giving her a brief hug. The word of praise given, Exelby went. Glowing, Jane trailed out after him.

'He was always the same,' muttered Sally Vause, helping Thomas off with his costume, now completely ready.

'Always?'

'Oh! He's no stranger to York, you know, though I notice he doesn't publicize it. It's all his past triumphs, for the media, but himself he never looks back. Always what he's doing next, that's our Bruce. But I remember. He came to the York Rep as a young actor. I believe he'd been in the Sheffield Playhouse company. He was here for a couple of seasons and then went off somewhere else. The next we heard he had gone into directing. Just as well. He was no sort of actor. Took what he wanted in the way of stage experience and when he might have been expected to be a mainstay for a year or two, off.'

'Do you remember all the small-time actors we've had here?'

'No. His name struck a bell and I got out my old theatre programmes. Then they reminded me.' Sally stitched vigorously at a length of woollen cloth.

'He wasn't much good, then?'

'I only actually remember him as Mole in *The Wind in The Willows*. He was wooden. Good-looking but no use as an actor at all. Top of the tree as a director though, I'll grant him that. I've grumbled about these costumes but they'll look terrific on set.'

In another part of the parish room were the Angels.

'I tell you he's wet,' said the plump blonde Angel sulkily. '"Call yourself a Devil," I said, "you ought to be one of those boring blessed Souls," I–'

'We all know what you said.' A thin dark Angel in glasses raised her head from Chaucer's *Canterbury Tales* which she was swallowing in much larger chunks than next year's O levels required. 'What we want to know is, why you said it?'

'I had an absolutely super idea to sabotage one of these boring rehearsals. I'd got one of Poison's tapes, the one the BBC banned because it's supposed to be all about drugs.'

'"Angels on a Trip", you mean?'

'That's it. Very appropriate, isn't it?' the blonde Angel giggled. 'I know he's pally with one of the music people and I told him to substitute the tape for one of theirs, wouldn't it have been a shriek? But he wouldn't do it. Said it wasn't worth being chucked out of the plays for.'

'It's you that's wet,' replied her friend. 'It would never have worked, they have all the tapes marked and numbered, and they'd spot it at once. It wasn't worth the row.'

'Who cares about the beastly plays anyway?'

'We do, and if you don't it's only because you were turned down for the BVM because you were too young,' said her friend with devastating candour.

The blonde Angel said two very rude unangelic words and took her mug for a refill of coffee.

'Don't drink too much,' warned Velvet.

As the director strode back to the set he saw Clare, the Virgin Mary, walking slowly with her script in her hand, folded open. She was looking first up and then down and muttering. Exelby stopped, which gave Jane Bugg the opportunity to catch up with him.

'You go on, Jane,' he said genially. 'See how everyone is getting on for me, will you?'

Then he moved to the Virgin's side.

50

'Problems?' His voice was gentle and understanding.

She blushed. 'Not really problems, Mr Exelby. I want to do credit to everyone who has faith in me for the part. I suppose I'm a little nervous, that's all.'

He took the book from her hands, his fingers brushing lightly over hers.

'Let me hear you.'

'Oh no, I couldn't possibly take up your time...'

'Please, Clare.'

She spoke some of her words nervously to his intent ear.

'Yes. Could be better. You seem a little lacking in self-confidence, my dear. After all you've been rehearsing some time now and all this should be perfect. I thought you knew your lines.'

'I do know them, Mr Exelby. I'm word-perfect. It's just nerves, and I'm worried over some of the emphasis.'

'A few of the cast go to have a drink after the rehearsal, don't they?'

'Yes.'

'Do you go?'

'Yes. I'm under age but I have an orange juice.'

'I'll join you tonight and we'll have a chat about it.'

With a reassuring smile he left her.

51

Night fell over the city.

In his caravan Poison Peters was alone. He had washed out his hair and it fell limply on to his shoulders. His face was bare, pallid and slightly pimply. He sat on his bed with his head bowed over the text of the plays, as he had been sitting for the past three hours. Sighing, he got up and went over to the tiny fitted fridge, lifted out the plateful of food he had bought and prepared earlier, and took off the cling film. There were some good cheese and varied salads. He put a carton of natural yoghurt ready on the flap table, and a bottle of untreated orange juice. The vodka bottle full of Malvern water stood on the small draining board.

He switched on the tape recorder to a low volume and the sound of medieval instruments filled the van.

After eating he washed up neatly and raised the blind to see the moonlit wall of the ancient ruins towering outside. He was in a triple-locked enclosure. Turning off the music, he let the silence wash through him. He felt, as he always did – and as an actor playing Christ must always do – completely and utterly alone. He undressed and slid into bed, a thin white radish. Closing his eyes he murmured, 'God, I'm not very good at saying this. But I need your help.' Then he was silent.

3

Mine enemies now will come nigh and draw
   near,
With all might they may, to mar my
   manhood.

The Cordwainers' Play

The next morning the hate mail began to
arrive. Both the director and the Christ
received a pile of it. 'You will burn in Hell,'
said one of the letters. As the whole lot was
delivered to the festival office, neither of
them was as yet aware of the infinite variety
of abuse, which was to become a feature of
their lives.

For the first time Poison Peters was on the
set of the mystery plays. He had been
heralded by a little flurry from the wings,
otherwise he might hardly have been noticed.
The road manager had left York – he had the
next tour to arrange – and Bruce Exelby was
on one side of Poison, the assistant stage
manager on the other; they walked forward
into view together.

Exelby was to put Poison through the
scenario. The set was quiet, although a
dozen people had arrived already. It was half

an hour before the technical rehearsal was due to begin. Sydney Absolom was fiddling with the lights. Thomas Churchyard was sitting sharing a flask of coffee with Humphrey Hale. The day was still warm and light, with the sun high.

'You appear here first,' said Exelby. Poison, a small slim figure in jeans, trainers and T-shirt, face devoid of make-up and hair falling limply about his head, climbed up the set after him.

'You wouldn't recognize him,' said Humphrey.

'No.' Thomas could hardly take his eyes from the insignificant figure. 'I didn't think he'd be able to wash all the stuff off his hair as easily as all that.'

'You've been taken in by appearances like everybody else.'

'Have I?' Tom pondered that. 'I wouldn't have said that I could be easily deceived. Of course I suppose I knew that he must look quite ordinary underneath.'

'No you didn't. No one expects a pop star to look ordinary, ever.'

For a while they both looked across at Bruce and Poison in silence. No acting was going on. Poison was only following Bruce from place to place, listening to his instructions, repeating phrases after him, opening and closing his arms, placing his feet, looking around now and again as if to memorize his positions in the complicated set. The younger man looked serious and concentrated, all his force drawn within himself. Thomas had to think a long time before he hit on the right word. Humility. That was it. The last thing one would ever associate with Poison Peters. Well, if he was conscious of his deficiencies, that was a good thing. He had never acted before and had only a few days to acquire what people spent years perfecting.

'When do you want the sound equipment ready?' shouted Sydney Absolom belligerently from the wings.

'As soon as you can, Sydney.'

'None of the others need amplification.'

'Poison is used to it.' There was no irritation on Exelby's part, but a firmness that invited no arguments. Absolom grunted and disappeared again. Bruce Exelby went into the shadow of a piece of mock wall in his wake. Their voices could be heard clearly.

'You've set the amplifier up here?'

'There isn't anywhere else to put it.'

'Hmmm – well, it'll do – but look, I don't want to be able to hear you moving about. I don't want to hear anything. No clicks, no footsteps. Nothing.' There were faint noises as Exelby examined the set-up.

'I'll put down a rubber mat.'

'All right. That should solve the problem. I don't want to hear a sound from you, Sydney.'

'I'll go home and fetch the mat.'

'When will you be ready to turn on? I want Poison to test it.'

'Later this evening.'

'OK.'

'I've got all the other electrics to look after, you know. This is just an extra burden.'

The two men emerged from behind the wall. Bruce clasped Sydney's thin bowed shoulder with a substantial hand.

'You'll do it.' He sounded suddenly jovial. 'I know I can rely on you, Syd.'

'I'll have to hurry or I won't be back for when you want to try the lights.' Absolom sounded reasonably mollified as he hurried off.

This was the night Sydney and his assistant were to give the lights their trial run, synchronized with the action. The technical rehearsal was the one the actors hated most. It dragged on and on while minor adjustments were made. Thomas assumed Syd had arrived back in time with his mat, because on cue the first spotlight lit up, and was followed by all the other lights in their elaborate sequence. The whole thing was jerky, because Absolom and his assistant were having to fit in with the action which was constantly stopping and starting as Exelby interfered, asking for one scene to be repeated, cajoling one actor, yelling at the Crowd, softly coaxing the Virgin Mary, joking with the group of little Devils and cursing the group of unco-operative sheep, who were proving almost as bad as the donkey.

There was no doubt that the director was singling out the Virgin Mary in a most marked way. Thomas wondered how her boyfriend felt about it. Flattery and praise were altering the girl; some of her dignified simplicity was wearing off, and she had taken to simpering at the director and making her gestures more elaborate and stagy. It wasn't an improvement.

The technics themselves seemed to be going rather well. Apart from the wrong spotlight being used in one scene, and trouble getting the right angle for the light beaming on the detached tower of stone on top of which the Archangel Michael made his dramatic appearance, there were no real hitches.

Poison had his script in his hand, but everyone else knew their lines by heart. Because of this perhaps, he seemed different; yet Thomas noticed that the slim pale figure drew the eye. He slid into place in the jigsaw with an ease and lack of commotion that Thomas, standing now in his archway in the sky, found rather surprising.

As the time wore on he noticed that Poison's hesitancy was falling from him. In the big speech in the Taylors' play Poison dropped the hand holding the script to his side, and obviously had the words by heart; his voice rose clearly and Thomas could hear every syllable. Suddenly the attention of the cast focused on their Christ as though a group of iron filings had swung to point at the pole. A power, thin yet and faint, seemed to radiate from him. 'I wonder if Exelby *did* make a mistake, after all? Or if Poison is going to be good?' thought Tom.

At last Exelby called a break.

'Got that amplifier fixed?' he asked Absolom. 'I want Poison to test it before we go any further. Set the mike up where he can use it during the Harrowing of Hell.'

'Right.' Absolom disappeared behind his spur of wall to switch on.

The amplifier and microphone were tested and all functioned perfectly with no problems. Everything else went off without any important hitches. On his high vantage point Thomas Churchyard felt happier and light in spirit, as the whole wonderful wheeling production turned through its sequences.

The only place where there was an uneasy pause came when the Christ had to be fastened to the cross and hang there suspended in centre stage for about twenty minutes, at the end of which the lights snapped off, leaving everything in darkness, while thunder rolled. During this dramatic darkness covering the moment of death the cross was lowered. The whole thing was a gruelling event for any actor. Poison Peters went through it well, considering that it was his first experience of the ordeal. Tom wondered whether he would not find it much worse when he was only dressed in a loin cloth. In that twenty minutes the air – summer though it was – would cool his body unbearably. He would hang almost naked and very uncomfortable, isolated, martyred, with a growing feeling of suffocation and light-headedness, in front of the gaping audience. The actors would be working away at their parts below him, separated from him as if by a void of miles and centuries.

After Poison had been lowered from the cross and was off-stage Thomas, who could see behind the wall of the abbey into the churchyard as well as in front of it on to the stage, noticed him rubbing his wrists and flexing his back and limbs to relieve them of tension.

On the whole it had been an encouraging rehearsal. If only those dratted sheep would behave themselves a bit better.

Sally Vause had been at the front, watching.

'At least there were no tantrums or hysterics,' she said to God as he was about to make his way home. 'He hasn't given much out – but most actors don't on a read-through. He'll have to work hard to learn his lines, but singers have to learn the words of their songs, I suppose, and perhaps the rest of the cast might carry the production.'

Tom looked at her in some surprise. 'I think he might turn out to be good, after all,' he said. 'How long have you been watching?'

'Oh, off and on. Velvet stayed in wardrobe.'

'I might be imagining things. But I think he might just possibly be very good indeed.' Tom put on his bicycle clips.

Sally looked after him indulgently.

It was during Poison's second rehearsal that Bruce Exelby was talking to the Virgin Mary.

'Still feeling unsure, Clare? Why don't I give you a little coaching? Are you free later?'

'Yes...'

'It might make all the difference. Contact your parents and tell them you'll be later than usual and we'll fit in an hour's tuition. Don't forget you've a career ahead of you, my girl! A good impression in this part will make all the difference in your student days – may make the difference between acceptance at a drama school and refusal.'

'Oh, Mr Exelby!'

'Bruce, please.' He nodded. 'See you later, then.'

When rehearsal was over, Clare was ready, clutching her lines to her bosom and all starry-eyed. Bruce Exelby came across her as though he had forgotten all about her –

put his hand to his forehead – said, 'Yes, of course!' – then added, 'I *will* make time for you, my dear – just give me a minute...'

She waited half an hour, while he spoke, it seemed, to everyone else in York. At last he came up to her and, taking her elbow in his hand in an avuncular way, walked along with her, talking.

'Where are we going, Mr Exelby?'

'Bruce, *please!* We theatricals, you know, must stick together ... the gatehouse seems quite a good place, don't you agree? Quiet and comfortable, which is all that's necessary to let us really concentrate on the words and their interpretation.'

The top floor of the gatehouse, St Mary's Lodge, was the flat which was available to the director of the mystery plays. They went up the stairs to it, Exelby dropping the latch behind them. He walked about switching on a lamp or two to counter the fading light outside, chatting briskly. He could really be very bright and amusing when he tried, telling stories of various productions. In the kitchen he made powdered coffee and brought Clare a mugful. She was on edge, but the casual handing to her of the thick workmanlike mug of hot liquid reassured her.

Exelby at last dropped down with an exhausted sigh in the chair opposite.

'Now to work!' he exclaimed.

She read, and he criticised, for some time. Exelby could be a patient and inspiring teacher, and he was that now. He made her move across the floor as she spoke the lines, and they thrashed out the relationships of words to movements, the thought and inner emotions conveyed.

'There is nothing better I can do than quote to you the words of Stanislavsky,' said Exelby. '"Out of the fusing of elements arises an important inner state which we call the inner creative mood." Once you learn how to achieve that you will be a superb actress. No, my dear, I am not flattering you. I believe it to be true. Now. It is late and I am tired.'

'I'll go at once!'

'No, no. I need a little refreshment. Won't you join me in a light supper?'

'Well … it would be a trouble to you…' Clare was dazzled by the situation. The director had the power of creating an atmosphere of sophistication, of giving her the feeling of being part of his world.

'I was only thinking of whipping up an omelette – a little French bread – a lettuce leaf or two–'

What could be more innocent, what could there be about that to cause her parents any worry?

'Perhaps your parents will be anxious if you stay out any longer. Give them a ring, the telephone is over there. I will of course take you home in the car.'

'It's only a step,' replied Clare, who lived in a big old house in Bootham Terrace. 'It is very kind of you. I would like an omelette very much. And I'm often out later than this.'

'Talk to me while I make it,' he asked.

'First put on a tape. You'll find them over there. I'll leave the door to the kitchen open and we can talk.'

She selected some softly wistful music and put it on. Now that the slight uneasiness of being alone for so long with a large and dominant male had passed and she felt quite safe, she began to feel a little provocative. The general mood relaxed. From the kitchen came a slight noise of cooking and table laying. Once she offered to help, but a cheerful 'No, no!' reassured her and kept her where she was, sitting by the tape deck and looking dreamily out of the window at the darkening sky.

'Come and get it!' came his voice at last.

On going into the kitchen she was surprised to find it almost in darkness and to see the table lit by two candles stuck on to saucers.

'I love candlelight, don't you?' he asked. 'And I've found a bottle. Do you drink, Clare? Or would you rather have a fruit juice? I find I sleep better after a little alcohol.'

Flattered, she agreed to have a glass of

wine. How pleasant it was to be on these easy friendly terms with the great director! He had a way of making her feel part, not of her little provincial world, but of an altogether wider and different one.

It was not until they had enjoyed a long and intimate meal and two glasses of wine each that – as she offered to help clear the table and they were both moving to and fro in the flickering light – he touched her. He slid a powerful arm around her waist and pulled her closer to him. At first Clare was stunned and her initial quiescence was read by Exelby as the assent which he had learned to expect in the women to whom he made his advances.

'Just a little kiss,' he murmured. 'You are so attractive...'

As his hands moved downwards over her hips and he bent to kiss her tempting young mouth Exelby was unprepared for the violent reaction which now came.

Clare suddenly realized her position and how carefully she had been manoeuvred into it. Apart from the fact that she was in love with her boyfriend she found the stubbly reddened face of the director repellent at such close quarters.

She jumped back violently, the mood of relaxation and provocation gone. '*No!*' she spat like a wildcat, her eyes suddenly alive and angry. She vibrated with horror and the shock of her awakening from the mood of easy undemanding companionship.

Before Exelby could remonstrate, could try to restore the cosy and propitious atmosphere, Clare had snatched up her playscript and had fled from the room. She stamped down the stairs as if each step was a personal enemy. She listened for hasty footsteps behind her but Exelby contented himself with standing at the top of the staircase and bellowing, 'Clare! Clare! Come back, you little fool!'

She was afraid that it would be impossible to get out of the door without returning and asking for the key, but it was only latched and opened easily. The wrought iron gates on to Marygate of course were closed. She ran back, half sobbing, to the wooden stair-ladder which led up the wall, built for the convenience of the players, chased up it and down the other side into the graveyard of St Olave's, thinking that from there she could get out on to Marygate. But after spending a full minute chasing round the church she realized that she could not.

Up and down the stair-ladder again – terrified that Bruce would come out of his tower-like dwelling and would catch her – she decided that the only way out was over the high gate. Blessing the long hours spent in the school gym, she shinned over the gate at the lowest part, placing her feet neatly between the vertical bars ... then she was safely outside the gardens and in the road, where she stood for a moment shaken and trembling.

She had not been pursued. Bending her head and crying a little she made her way home and slipped upstairs without seeing her parents, only calling out that she was in and was going straight to bed and had had a hot drink, thank you.

The accident did not happen until Poison's third rehearsal.

The feeling against him in the city was stronger and more vociferous than ever, now that it appeared he had not been frightened away, but was likely to remain and actually act.

Everyone on the set itself had relaxed a little. Poison had stopped carrying his script and hardly ever forgot his lines. Exelby was beginning to work on him to bring out his own unique interpretation of the role. It seemed, after the worries of a week before, almost incredible that the plays were progressing as normally as they were. The sheep were still, at the moment, causing the most problems. The assistant stage manager was tired of clearing up after them, but didn't like to delegate the job to anyone else.

It had been noted as a strange thing that the person playing Christ in some way seemed set apart; it always happened. The rest of the cast were inclined to treat him, as time went on, almost with reverence. It may just have been that after spending so many hours looking up to him on stage, the feeling was hard to dispel. But it is certain that the Christ always acquires authority.

Thomas could not have said that he found the part of God enlivening. It was rather static. He spoke from the archway in the sky which had once been the centre window of the wall of the ancient abbey, and when not speaking was either standing there looking impressive or sitting on the wooden walk-way behind the medieval masonry. It did give him a bird's-eye view of the action, and it did give him the chance to sit out of sight and talk in whispers to the Angel Gabriel if enough noise was going on below to drown the sound.

Humphrey Hale always brought up his hip flask of whisky and a good book; the book to while away the time and the whisky to keep him warm. The plays began as the sun started to go down in splendour in the western sky and the arches were outlined black against it; then, as the performance wore on, the time came when the floodlights illumin-ated the arches and they in turn were light against the blackness of the night sky. By then Humphrey could no longer see to read, and the bottle came into its own.

This was the first of the three dress rehearsals.

All went as well as any rehearsal ever does. Exelby lost his temper rather fewer times than usual. The only unpleasant episode came between the director and the Virgin. After all his buttering up, she had definitely got a little above herself; it had gone to her head and she had begun to behave like the star of the production. But the way he treated her was hardly justified.

'Do you have to behave like that?' he suddenly barked at her, and as she jerked round and looked at him in surprise: 'Heaven save me from amateurs! What the hell do you think you're doing, girl? You're supposed to be the Mother of God, for heaven's sake, not a wooden doll strutting across the stage. You're useless. Absolutely useless. Get off. Is your understudy here? Anyone's performance would be better than this.'

'What's wrong?' faltered Clare.

'Wrong? I can't imagine why you ever thought you could act. What made you come for audition?'

'But you chose me, Mr Exelby – you said – you've said lots of times – RADA – the West End–'

'Never mind what I said.' His voice was a snarl, nothing else. It hissed out so clearly that the most distant person must have heard. One of the gardens' regular inhabitants, a peacock, began to call hoarsely as if in response.

'It's what I'm saying now that matters. As for RADA they'd as soon have a girl from behind a supermarket counter as you. Better in fact. At least she might be able to look intelligent. You either improve in the next two minutes or you're *off* and I mean *off*.'

Thomas heard afterwards that the tears overflowed from Clare's eyes and ran down her cheeks, clear crystal drops, hardly marking the soft pinkness, leaving her eyes unsullied, not reddened, only washed and sparkling. Tears such as only the young can shed. She was shaking. She acted on bravely, commanding her voice and quelling its quavering.

'For God's sake!' Exelby exclaimed irritably, once or twice. The whole cast had gone quiet. If Clare was in trouble none of them was safe. The director said nothing else about sending her off, but at the end of that part there was no final word of praise, no hastening over to pat her hand. He ignored her, contrary to his recent practice, as she walked off the stage.

The scene had so shaken the rest of the cast that they acted as though mesmerized. For once their thoughts were not centred on Poison Peters. It was with a conscious effort that Thomas turned his thoughts back to Poison, as the time came for Christ's first long speech.

Thomas saw Poison approach the microphone. From his viewpoint he could only see the singer's back. By noticing the movement of his arm, he had no doubt Poison was reaching out, as he usually did, to slightly adjust the mike. He seemed to do it automatically, however recently he had adjusted the mike before.

It was obvious at once that something was wrong. Even from behind and above, Thomas could see that. Poison did not at once drop his hand and launch into the speech. His whole figure went rigid, clenched, and no words came.

Exelby was out front, looking up at the stage and Poison Peters. As Thomas left his high window arch and began to run along the wooden walkway and down the ladder Exelby also moved. The singer appeared to be frozen onto the microphone, still and voiceless.

'I knew he'd be on drugs,' came a disgusted voice from the Crowd.

As Exelby ran across the stage towards the singer he tripped over the microphone cable, almost went sprawling, then recovered himself. Simultaneously Poison Peters's body seemed to give a great jerk like a hooked fish leaping out of the water, and he flew through the air across the stage. He crashed into the stones of the abbey wall and fell down helplessly, sprawling like a rag doll.

'Don't anybody touch anything!' yelled Exelby. He ran to the singer, reaching him at the same time as Thomas Churchyard hurled himself panting from the bottom of the ladder onto the stage near the place where Peters had been thrown.

Exelby bent over Poison Peters. Poison's golden brown eyes were open and aware.

'I'm all right,' he croaked.

'You're alive. Thank God. I'll kill that electrician.'

Flinging away, Exelby rushed to the hidden place where Absolom was sitting serenely on his rubber mat, adjusting the amplifier. Taking one look at him, Exelby rushed to the plug which connected the amplifier to the mains and threw the switch. Only then did he turn on Sydney Absolom.

'You've done it this time,' he shouted at the top of his voice. Turning to the assistant stage manager who had been running close behind him, he ordered: 'Fetch the police and an ambulance at once.'

'What?' Absolom looked up for the first time from his amplifier. 'What have you turned the juice off for? That drug addict of yours wants the mike. Too weak to make his voice heard without it.' Making a great show of indignation he walked towards the plug.

'Don't you touch that!' shrieked Exelby as he grabbed Absolom's arm. 'It's lethal. Oh,

71

hell,' letting go of the arm – almost throwing it away from him – 'touch it if you want. You're expendable. You do what you want to yourself. But you've just nearly killed Peters. It's no thanks to you that he isn't dead.'

'Nearly killed...?'

'Your bloody equipment is live. You've just about killed him!'

Sydney Absolom went white. 'What do you mean? If anything was wrong I would have known. I was handling the stuff.'

'Oh yes, on your little rubber mat! Set it up nicely, haven't you? Well, don't think you're going to get away with it.' Exelby took hold of the older man once more, in a vicious grip. He dragged him out on to the stage, towards the spot where Thomas was standing guard over Poison and waving back the Crowd who had rushed over to see what was going on.

'Good man, Churchyard. Do you think he ought to go to hospital? I've sent the ASM to ring for an ambulance. Have we got a first aider around?'

'I'll be all right,' came a thread of a voice from Poison. 'Just get me back to the caravan to rest a bit.'

'Not a bad idea,' said Tom to Exelby.

'Right. Can you help him? I'm not letting go of this murdering bastard.'

'I'm not a murderer,' said Absolom in a

72

voice almost as faint as the singer's.

'He's been Across,' said Exelby. 'Have *you* ever been Across? Know what it's like? Another few seconds could have killed him. I've never been Across but I know a few who have. Oh yes, it was easy for you to arrange, wasn't it?'

Thomas knelt down by the singer and slid an arm under him. Until now there had been no movement of any part of the thin body except the lips and eyes, since he had flown through the air and crashed against the wall. Thomas eased him upward. Poison's legs seemed too weak to support him, but after a few seconds he was standing, leaning heavily on Thomas.

'I think you ought to go to hospital.'

'No thanks. The caravan will do. Will you help me there?'

They set off, Tom half carrying the singer, who staggered the few steps off the stage and through the opening in the abbey wall. The caravan was only yards away. Thomas came to a decision. He didn't say anything. He just turned towards Poison and picked him up in his arms. Poison lay passively across his chest, legs and arms dangling, his head bowed on to Thomas's shoulder. They looked like Michelangelo's 'Pieta'.

The actors who saw them drew back, shocked and awe-inspired. Only one person, Sue Brown, the assistant director, rushed ahead to the caravan door. It was locked.

'Pocket,' whispered Poison, and Sue felt in his jeans pocket for the key. It seemed minutes before she managed the lock. Then Thomas climbed the two steps and slid sideways through the door with his load.

Like all caravans there wasn't much room, but what space there was was clean and tidy. A bed with a checked wool cover was made up under the end window.

Lowering Poison's legs to the floor, Thomas flipped back the bedcovers with his left hand and then set the slim body on the edge of the bed. He bent down and un-fastened the trainers, slipped them off Poison's feet and then raised the thin legs and slid him into the bed. Poison settled his head on the pillow with a sigh of relief, and Thomas stood erect and looked down at the pale face.

'I'd better get you something.'

'I'll be all right now I'm in bed.'

'You need some kind of stimulant. Brandy or something.'

'A cup of sweet tea,' suggested Poison.

Thomas now had time to look round the caravan. He had pictured it as a den of iniquity and expected it to be stinking and revolting. Instead it was immaculate, and smelled pleasantly of the bunch of culinary herbs stuck in a jam jar on the tiny worktop. He began rapidly to open cupboard doors.

There were no bottles of either wine or spirits, certainly no brandy. Remembering the vodka bottle he had seen Poison swig from, Tom looked for that and found it at last, but empty. Perhaps a cup of sweet tea would be as good as anything. He didn't like the look of the closed eyes and the white face on the pillow. He found the kettle, half full of water, and the small stove and a box of matches. In seconds the kettle was on and beginning to sing as Thomas searched for some tea. He found Earl Grey and a small china teapot. Spooning it in lavishly he next looked around for sugar. There was some in a delicate fluted china basin which matched the teapot and cups and saucers.

Stirring the tea madly Thomas wondered how long he dared leave it to brew. Poison had not spoken for what seemed like hours. No doubt the doctor would arrive any minute. Thomas poured a cup of tea, sweetened it, and added skimmed milk from a carton in the fridge. It looked very much as if Poison was on a cure of some kind. He could hardly be slimming.

Raising Poison to a sitting position Tom held the cup to his lips.

'I'm not a baby, you know,' said the singer.

'I couldn't find any spirits,' Tom sounded apologetic.

'You won't. There aren't any.'

'I thought … you insisted on being alone

in a caravan so that you could behave how you liked.'

'That's right.'

'I don't see...'

'Look, for heaven's sake keep quiet about this. How I live is my own affair, right?'

'Right.'

'A word to anybody and you're for it.'

Poison had taken the cup of tea in a trembling hand. 'You've made this strong, haven't you? Don't you know Earl Grey is supposed to be drunk weak without milk and sugar?'

'The sugar is for shock.'

'Well – you didn't have to put milk in it – still, I'm grateful. Thanks and all that.'

'I'm just puzzled about the drink.'

'It's none of your business. Well – if you don't let it out! I'll skin you alive if you do and then deny anything you've said. I've never been able to touch alcohol and that's the top and bottom of it. It makes me ill.'

'But all the drunkenness?'

'That's the line, isn't it, yeah?'

'All that being sick on stage?'

Poison grimaced. 'That was the time I did try some, to see if I'd grown out of the reaction. I was as sick as a pig, all over the stage. Aaaah! Still it was good for business and all that.'

'What do you drink, then?'

'Milk – Malvern water – and Earl Grey

tea, but weaker than this stuff.' Poison made a face and took a few more sips from the cup. 'Don't you dare tell anyone.'

'My lips are sealed.'

A knock came at the door, then it opened and a man came in, pink-faced, wearing a suit and carrying the kind of briefcase doctors use.

'Dr Belcombe,' he said. 'I'm told Mr Peters has had a powerful electric shock. Been Across, as they say, the main current. He ought to be in hospital.'

'I'm alive,' said Poison, 'and if I was in hospital the place would get besieged. I'll be quieter here. I'll be all right soon.'

It was still a struggle for him to speak, the words came out with an obvious effort, and Thomas regretted talking to him earlier. The singer's forehead was covered with a fine sweat. He fell back on his pillow exhausted.

'You escaped death by seconds.'

'Crashing against that wall didn't half hurt.'

'Let's be sure there's nothing broken.'

'I'm going,' said Thomas. 'Perhaps you could report his condition to Mr Exelby, doctor.'

Thomas walked away slowly, thinking about Poison Peters, the drunken pop star who was made sick by the smallest amount of alcohol. Back on stage he found the place bristling with policemen.

'The rehearsal's off,' Humphrey Hale told him. 'The little Devils and Mary and the sheep have gone home already. Everyone else is going now.'

'They won't want me, then.'

'Oh yes they do. Our Bruce is screaming that this is a case of attempted murder. He and Absolom have gone to Fulford Road police station and you've got to follow them.'

'Why me?'

'Because you were noticing what happened – otherwise you wouldn't have got down that ladder so fast.'

The seven little Devils were supposed to have gone home, but they had other things to do. What was the point of going home tamely when the Angels were still about? On one or two nights they had had quite a good time making frightening ghostly noises around the church and the Angels had responded quite satisfactorily...

'I dare you,' one of them said to Christopher, the biggest of the seven.

'All right, I will, then.'

'What's he going to do?' asked Nicholas as Christopher ran off into the dusk.

'Oh, only lever up one of the tops of the tombs. It'll really scare the girls. We've all got to be ready to groan.'

Christopher returned, and set to work on

the heavy stone slab, while the others groaned and moaned, and the Angels shrieked and clutched each other nearby.

'What on earth are you doing?' asked a cool voice from the darkness. It was Velvet Smith.

'Just playing...'

'Come along this minute and get your costumes off. You'll spoil them.'

The Angels came obediently. The Devils scattered and ran wildly in all directions at once, shouting, rattling sticks, and one of them creating a metallic fusillade on some iron railings...

'I don't understand what all this is about,' said Sydney Absolom. He was sitting miserably in an interview room at the police station.

'It's about this,' said Bob Southwell. The amplifier, microphone, and all the rest of the sound equipment were in the corner, and he pointed graphically to the plug, which had been placed on the table. His glasses flashed with reflected light, as if they too were accusing. 'Do you usually wire things up so that they will electrocute people you don't like?'

'I don't know what you mean.' Defensively.

'You know the actor, Mr Peters, had a near-fatal accident earlier this evening?'

'I've been told so, yes. I wouldn't have known about it otherwise.'

'He reached out to adjust the microphone – apparently it's a habit of his – and was wrapped across the main circuit and unable to tear himself away. Fortunately Mr Exelby, in rushing to his assistance, tripped over the microphone cable and by so doing must have pulled out the microphone plug from the amplifier and broken the current. Mr Peters's muscles then went into spasm, he was hurled back from the microphone and crashed into the stone wall a few feet away.'

Sydney Absolom said nothing, although there was a pause in which he could have interjected some of the mad words which were reeling round in his head.

'So we were called to the scene to investigate the cause of the accident. I came along because we were told it was a case of attempted murder. And we found this' – he gestured again at the plug – 'with the earth wire unconnected and touching the live pin. Who wired this plug, Mr Absolom?'

He gulped. 'I did.'

'Well? Do you want to make a statement?'

Sydney Absolom swallowed again, hard, as if he was trying to digest his Adam's apple. He nodded.

A minute or two later a constable was sitting, ballpoint at the ready, and another constable had brought Sydney Absolom a cup of tea. Bob Southwell had taken pity on his white and horrified face, and began to reconsider his first assumption that this was a deliberate attempt to harm Poison Peters.

'We don't usually have sound amplification in the mystery plays,' began Absolom. 'I've done the lights on the last two plays. So I was chosen to do them on this one again. Everything went all right until Mr Exelby announced his Christ.'

'You were very much against his choice?'

'I was – I am – yes. That doesn't mean I'd try to kill him!'

'You have been heard to make threats, Mr Absolom.'

Sydney bent his head. 'Yes.'

'Go on with your story.'

'Because P – Mr Peters was our Christ, and Mr Exelby wasn't sure about the strength of his voice, he wanted the amplifier and mike. The road manager brought it and the mikes and everything. I was expected to fix it up in a hurry. They wanted to test it straight away and see how it worked in the open air, so I had to connect it up. Then I found it had a modern continental-type plug and the power sockets are an older style. Luckily I had an older-type plug in my odds-and-ends box.' There was a note of pride in his voice, the note common to handymen with odds-and-ends boxes. 'When I tried to

81

fix it to the amplifier there was a slight problem – there were only two retaining screws for the three wires of the main flex. So I used those to fasten down the live and neutral wires, just to get the amplifier working.'

'And what did you do with the earth lead?' asked Bob Southwell in a noncommittal voice.

'Well, that was a problem. I thought I'd have to search for a third screw later. So for the time being I rested it inside the plug top with its bare end near the earth pin.'

'And you think that was safe?'

Absolom spoke to his fingers, which were resting on the edge of the table. 'It was only temporary. I switched on and tested the amplifier and microphone, and everything functioned perfectly. Mr Peters used the microphone that night and all was well.'

'Did you find a third screw?'

Absolom made another remark, very low, to his fingers. 'I forgot all about it.'

'Oh, I see! You forgot all about it. You have a bare wire loose in a plug and forget all about it. This is the perfect murder plot, is it not? You sit secure on your little rubber mat. The play goes on. Inside your safe-looking plug the plastic covering on the earth wire twists and flexes as plastic coverings do. Sooner or later the set-up is going to become lethal and Poison Peters is going to get hold of it. This man you've been making threats against. He's the only one who uses the microphone, isn't he?'

'Anyone might have touched it,' said Absolom.

'True. Every time you switched on it was like a time bomb which might kill someone at any minute. Including you.'

'Yes. It looks like that.'

'Looks like that! It damn well was like that. It was a murder plot aimed at Poison Peters but liable to kill anyone at all at any time.' The large lenses of his glasses were filled with reflections of the lamp on the table and his thoughts could not be read.

'I never wanted to kill anyone,' muttered Absolom.

'You nearly did. A few seconds more and you would have.'

Absolom began to cry, bending his head on to his hands, his narrow shoulders shaking.

'All right,' said Bob Southwell after a few minutes. 'We've had all the equipment and the plug looked at by a local expert in electrical things. He says it was stupidity and inefficiency and that it doesn't look like a murder attempt.'

'You just said it was,' sniffled Absolom.

'It might well have been. If Poison had died do you think I'd be able to let you go?'

'Can I go?'

'Yes.' Tiredly. 'Though Mr Exelby would

rather I kept you in irons in a padded cell.'

'I'll get that third screw now.'

'I'm afraid you're off the job. You are not to be allowed on to the set of the plays again, and I must warn you that if you try to go there, or make any contact with the cast, or make any more threats against either Mr Exelby or Mr Peters, then I will have to take a much more serious view of the whole incident than I am doing today.'

The Youngest Shepherd and Clare, the Virgin Mary, were still sitting in a quiet corner of the public house on Marygate. So far all she had done was cry quietly and all he had done was glower at her. Now everyone but them had departed, the landlord was washing the glasses, and casting glances in their direction.

'What was it all about, then?' he said at last.

Very quietly, and with her handkerchief still at her eyes, she told him all about the previous night's happenings.

'I'll kill him,' said the Youngest Shepherd fervently.

'Oh, no, David, you mustn't. Please don't be so angry. Nothing *happened*, you know. I'm still ... what I'm supposed to be.'

'You'd better be.'

'Oh, yes, David, I'm waiting for ... us ... you know ... when the time comes.'

'I want to marry a virgin,' said David, who

84

liked to dominate exclusively over Clare.

'Oh, yes, David.'

'Come on. I'll walk you home.'

Poison Peters was kneeling by his bed in the caravan. The text of the plays lay near to him. Closed, under his left hand, was a copy of the Bible, which he had read for the first time since arriving in York. He was trying to pray.

'Lord God, I'm not good at this. I can't remember how you're supposed to do it.' Words and phrases from school assemblies ran round his head like half-heard music. 'But like I said before, if I am to carry out this task Thou hast put before me, then I need Thy help. Today I nearly came to You. Bruce Exelby said I'd "been Across". It nearly finished me and I'll never be the same again. It's so close, the dividing line. It's so quick – the time needed to cross it. Death and I have shaken hands.'

He stopped and there was not a sound except the whirling of his thoughts.

His language became more archaic as he remembered words and phrases which seemed the right ones to use.

'I always thought it a great honour, Lord, to be asked to represent Thy Son. Now I have been very close to Thee. Please let this experience help me to be worthy. I am but a miserable … what … worm, one of Thy creatures; and if one of Thy creatures, can I be other than part of Thy glory? I pray that this miserable worm be allowed in some sort to figure forth the image of Thy Son...'

His little stock of words exhausted, he knelt on with bent head, closed eyes and calm hands, motionless as they lay separately on the coverlet. The night deepened outside. The gates of the Museum Gardens were locked. High in the tower of St Mary's Lodge by the St Olave Gate burned the lights of Bruce Exelby's flat. Above the deep shadows, the heaps of blackness which were the trees, the jet shadows of the walls of St Mary's Abbey, were other gleams of light. The floodlighting which lit up the city, the yellow lights of the roads which ringed it, wove a golden cocoon high in the air, a cocoon of silk-like threads of light as if York were a holy city, and as if the depths of night resting within were a holy sleep – a sleep within which vigils and consecrations might take place.

4

Now raise him nimbly. Heave and Ho!
And set him by this mortice here,
And let him fall down at one blow–
For sure that pain will have no peer,
Heave up – let down! All his bones so
Are sundered everywhere.
The Pinners' and Painters' Play

Thomas next saw Robert Southwell the following day when he went home after work before attending the second dress rehearsal.

'I was wondering what you're going to do about all the threatening letters,' he said diffidently, not wanting to sound as if he was teaching the police their job.

Bob looked up from his weeding at the sound of the deep, authoritative voice. 'How did you hear about them? I'm doing nothing,' he said, pulling up a dandelion and scrutinizing its root. 'It's all sound and fury.'

'But yesterday?'

'Pure accident.'

'Well, I don't think poor old Sydney would actually try to harm anyone. He looked very crestfallen when I took him home.' Even Absolom's fluffy cloud of hair had seemed to join in his general dejection, drooping about his ears.

'It's easy to think there is danger when there is none. We're checking the hate mail in case any of the letter-writers really seem serious, and keeping it all for the time being. Exelby and Peters are both getting a fair amount.'

'You aren't putting a guard on Poison Peters?'

'No need.'

Tom felt disappointed. Things to do with the police were not as dramatic as he expected. There was an amused glint in Bob's spectacles.

Thomas put on his costume and make-up in the parish room of St Olave. The next day the props and costumes for the principals were going to be taken up to the superior dignity of the Tempest Anderson Hall, which was much nearer to the place of performance and more private. Only the lesser fry – the Crowd, the Devils and the Soldiers – would remain based in the parish room. This was the only time he would have to take the rather embarrassing walk in full costume up Almery Lane, across Marygate, and in through the St Olave's Gate.

Thomas mounted the set of wooden steps which had been built from the Museum Gardens up the wall which divided the gardens from St Olave's churchyard, and then walked down the corresponding set on the other side of the wall, finding himself in the graveyard. It was shadowed by its beautiful trees and full of medieval people in colourful clothes, sitting or leaning on the tombs, their vast garments draped over the chill stones.

A great deal of cheerfulness was to be sensed, in spite of the tension inseparable from a dress rehearsal. Soldiers and the mothers of the Innocents they were shortly to massacre were fraternizing in a manner which would have worried Herod. Lucifer was offering a cigarette to one of the Crowd whom he was later to drive screaming into Hell. Humphrey Hale, the Archangel Gabriel, had lifted his nose out of his book and was chatting to a scantily dressed Eve. Michael the Archangel was complaining about the weight of his flaming sword to the props mistress, who had a little tent in which all manner of things were being looked after, mended, altered, as the situation demanded. She could hardly move in there for the piles of willow branches which had been freshly cut, ready to serve as palms during the entry into Jerusalem.

It seemed as if the near-accident the evening before had had a cathartic effect; everyone was less nervy than they had been.

'Is Poison all right?' Thomas asked Jane Bugg. 'Has he got over the shock?'

'He seems to be fine. He was here a minute ago with dear *Bruce*. Even *Bruce* looks cheerful.'

Jane, the large medieval lady whom nobody could stand, was one of the clerical staff attached to the engineering division in the office where Tom worked every day. It was a pity she was such a know-all. Underneath he was sure she was all right. She even looked better in a wimple than when one could see her hair strained back over her head to make a minute knob at the top rear of her skull. She went on in her crass voice, 'I don't know if he's planning to let Peters off the Crucifixion tonight, until he's had more time to recover.'

Thomas had hardly looked round for his friends before Bruce Exelby appeared again, purposeful and dominating – even brutal, bull-headed, bruising, in his attitude that day.

'Everyone ready? Good. Musicians, take your places. Everyone else, to your starting positions. Crowd, I don't want to hear you. Of course it isn't much fun to stand and wait but that doesn't mean you've got to rhubarb rhubarb while you're doing it. God, your throne is in position now on the platform centre top. Would you go up there please instead of in the window? You can come down and do what you like when you're not on. I want to know at the end of your first stint whether you're happy with the arrangement.'

The throne, resplendent with gold paint, had been placed on a specially built platform on the very top centre of the remaining abbey wall, on one of the places where it corbelled out to support gothic vaulting which had long since vanished. 'It's lucky I don't mind heights,' thought Thomas as he seated himself high in the sky in front of the sunset. He was aware of majesty descending on him like a mantle.

Feeling strangely remote in his position, Thomas declaimed his great opening speech and then moved into the interplay with Lucifer. The wide set was peopled only by Angels and Seraphs and the Devils, who, led by their infernal Lord, went tumbling down the long slope which had been built on one side of the stage, as in a moment of high drama they were precipitated into the red-lit masonry arch of Hell's mouth.

'You're no bloody good up there for that scene,' Exelby yelled up at Thomas. 'Too far away. Your voice gets lost. Save the throne for the end. Go on using the window arch for the beginning.'

'Right.'

The production moved smoothly into the plays of the Cardmakers, Fullers, and Coopers, which three had been amalgamated in Canon Purvis's modern translation into one play of Adam and Eve and the Fall, indicating the necessity for the Redemption. Among their Eden of stitched felt leaves the slender and beautiful ancestors of man were a pair of delightfully touching young lovers.

To those sitting out front Thomas Churchyard's voice, echoing with its fine resonance, speaking out in love as well as anger the condemnation of Adam and Eve, brought suddenly home the whole allegorical meaning of the Fall of Man.

God now descended from his window arch and went to sit in the front of the stage. It was the only time he was going to have the opportunity of seeing some of the production from the point of view of the audience. He particularly liked the next bit – the Spicers', Pewterers' and Founders', Tile Thatchers', Chandlers', Goldsmiths', and Marshalls' Plays, which took the action through the conception and birth of Christ.

He loved the symbolic birth, where Mary bent over, in the vast circle of her blue cloak, then unfolded herself and lifted up her arms like wings, revealing the infant child in her lap. Then came the Shepherds with their recalcitrant sheep, who seemed to be learning their parts at last, and the pathos of the flight into Egypt.

The time now came for Jesus's baptism, which was Poison's first entrance, and a feeling of heightened expectancy ran through the whole cast and those elsewhere on the set. He came, a figure in a simple white woollen gown which fell into natural medieval folds, and with his first words, 'John, all mankind is frail,' which rang out clear as the voice of a bird, the plays, powerful as they had been before, moved into a wholly greater dimension. Thomas Churchyard, recognizing an extraordinary stage presence, also recognized subconsciously that this man had no need of amplifying equipment to make his voice carry to the farthest seat on the staging.

From this point in the Barbers' Play, the action moved smoothly through the Locksmiths', the Cap Makers', and the Skinners' Plays, before breaking for the interval after the wonderful entry into Jerusalem, the triumphant high point where Christ, on the ass which had earlier taken Mary down the slope on her flight into Egypt, now ascended the same long slope, leading up through flat areas and flights of steps crowded with happy cheering colourful people waving their palm branches.

He thought Bruce Exelby could have nothing but praise for such a first half. But the director, striding on stage and looking out of place in his modern dress, had plenty of faults to find. 'And we'll get it right if we have to stay here all night,' he announced ominously.

Thomas saw the Virgin Mary trembling,

and felt that he could not bear to see her publicly disgraced again. Getting up hastily he went round to the back of the set and climbed the ladder on to the walkway which ran behind the window arches. He might be wanted and woe betide anyone who was not ready to jump instantly at the director's word.

After this beginning the fault finding was not all that bad; there were details Exelby didn't like and couldn't think how they had crept in, even if he had ordered them himself the day before. No one was likely to point that out or contradict him. There were faults and hesitancies which were remarked on scathingly. No one was praised. A good many people, including the Virgin Mary, were made to feel that they had got off lightly from heinous sins.

Then suddenly the mood changed; all was sweetness and light. 'Coffee for everyone,' Exelby declared, and happy chattering began. The Soldiers broke ranks and managed to be first in the queue for coffee.

But instead of going better after Exelby's exhortations, everything went worse. The sudden sunniness had only been the smile on the face of the tiger. People forgot their lines and their positions right through the Cutlers' and the Cordwainers' Plays; it was not until the Bowyers' and Fletchers' that they began to get back into the swing they had attained in the first half.

Yet Tom Churchyard, who had again ventured to sit in the front, had to admit that there had been some truth in all Exelby's criticisms, though they would not have occurred to him. But that was what a director was for, after all. That was his job, to see the faults no one else had noticed and do something about them. The Tapestry Makers', the Cooks' and Waterleaders', the Tile Makers', the Shermans' Plays progressed; Christ was condemned.

Now came the Pinners' and Painters' Play, in which Christ is crucified. Exelby had said no word to the contrary, so Thomas supposed he must consider Poison fit enough for the ordeal. Remembering the dead weight of the young man in his arms the previous day – his white face on the pillow – Tom thought he would have got someone else to do that bit today. What were understudies for if they did nothing?

Meanwhile Poison was journeying ever upward to the place of execution, carrying his cross. In this production two crosses were used. The cross on which he was actually crucified was left permanently on the highest stage area. During most of the performance it lay back at an angle, its head resting on a support pole. It was only when Christ was firmly fixed on it that it was raised up to the vertical. It could be seen by the audience, particularly in the highest tiers of seats, but their attention was always on the action, and it was hardly noticed that Poison carried a different and lighter cross, for which he was truly thankful. The lightweight cross was discreetly disposed of by a group of actors before the crucifixion itself, being lowered inconspicuously down the back of the set.

Poison lay down on the cross, which was at an angle of thirty-five degrees. He placed his feet on the footrest, a meagre few inches of wood projecting from the upright. He put his fingers on either side of the bolt projecting from the crossbeam, the bolt which was meant to look as though it penetrated his hand, but which he would have to clutch as time dragged on. Then he did the same with the other hand. He was wearing only a loincloth by this time. Pieces of white cloth were bound strongly round his wrists and ankles and hips to help take his weight. Then came the moment for him to be lifted upright.

All the soldiers began to heave, and the cross rose.

'Stop!'

The voice came, it seemed, from the earth, the very ground.

The soldiers were still tugging. Their job was almost done. Another few degrees…

'Stop! You must stop!' came again, loud

and desperately. The cross shifted in a way no one had expected. It lurched about two feet downwards, and there was a cracking sound.

The soldiers dropped the cords they had been pulling to raise the cross and rushed forward, grabbing at it, two on each side.

'What the hell is happening?' cried Bruce Exelby.

Tom, seeing that something was wrong, jumped up from the front seat he had been occupying and dashed across the grass to where the built-up set began, up one of the flights of stairs, to the base of the upper stage. There were several archways which led underneath the wooden structure, which had been made to look like an extension of the ancient ruined walls themselves. He dived into the nearest arch, at the same time as several other onlookers.

It was dark under the upper stage, but light filtered in through the various openings, and a shaft of light beamed down the hole for the foot of the cross. One plank of the staging, the exact width of the cross, hinged back to allow the movement of the cross. When the cross was raised to the vertical, the plank was lowered to form an additional rear support for it, and to prevent anyone accidentally stepping into the narrow slot. It was through this slot that the desperate voice of the ASM had risen to the soldiers above.

The assistant stage manager had the unenviable task of waiting down here until the moment came for him to fasten the cross firmly in position. A board was locked to the scaffolding under the upper stage, and the foot of the cross was fastened to this with an ordinary half-inch bolt which acted as a pivot. Once the Christ was fastened on to the cross as it lay in the sloped back position, it was raised upright pivoting on this bolt. When the ASM pushed a second, higher, bolt into position through cross and board, it was secure. Last of all the plank on the stage above was lowered.

With upstretched hands which looked tiny and fragile against the thick wood the ASM was trying to support the base of the cross.

'Well?' said Thomas, panting.

'Get Peters off the cross,' cried the ASM. 'The pivot has given way. The whole thing shot downwards. Look at it now! It's caught on that cross pole of the scaffolding, or it would have crashed down at once.'

Tom could see. One edge of the base of the cross had just come into contact with a round scaffold pole on its lurch downwards, and looked as if the slightest jar would make it slip off the smooth cylindrical surface.

'Can we push something underneath to support it?'

'If someone can fetch a lump of wood or something…'

'Is it safe to touch him at all until we've supported the base?'

'No – but he must be got off. And without moving the cross. Another movement however slight and it will come crashing down here out of control, with him on it.'

Sweat broke out on Thomas's forehead and the hairs went up on the back of his neck. He could think of nothing that could be done to stop a tragedy. The slot in the stage was only a few inches wide; if cross and actor came down together, the combined weight and impetus – for it was tall – would break Poison's legs and probably his spine, if it did nothing worse.

'Can you support the cross up there and stop it sliding down? It mustn't move at *all*, not a fraction!' he shouted, hoping that his strong voice would carry up through the hole and the shaft of light to the soldiers clutching the cross. 'Some of you hold it *firmly* and others get Peters off.'

There was a noise from the stage as though the people up there had understood and were acting on his words. Bruce Exelby came charging into the dark crowded space under the stage.

'My God,' he said softly, picking up a piece of the broken bolt from the floor. 'This isn't an accident. The iron bolt didn't snap. This isn't iron at all. It is a bloody bit of wood, broken in two... Get the police.'

'Get Peters off first,' retorted Tom, holding the bottom of the cross as well as he could to help the ASM. Not that their hands could have stopped its downward movement if the whole heavy thing had begun to shift. He looked at the smooth surface of the scaffold pole, and the narrow edge of the cross, which had rested on it and stopped the downward progress.

Thomas could see that the thing in the director's hands was not iron at all but a broken bit of wood. And when he looked at the end of the cross he saw the rest of it protruding from the pivot-hole; a round stick like a branch of willow, only thicker than the willow wands which were used as palms.

'I'll get the police my bloody self,' said Exelby, and went.

It had taken a long time to tie Poison to the cross, and it took longer to get him off, for he was high up now, and the actors hardly dared move for fear of setting the contraption sliding. The soldiers, who had been chosen for their strong and heavy appearance, were trying to hold it firmly on either side, and several of the Crowd had come rushing up and were gingerly pulling at the white cloth strips round Poison's feet.

'We want a step ladder,' someone said.

Poison said nothing.

If he had had any colour in his face to start with it would have gone, but he looked very little different. He was biting his bottom lip and holding on grimly to the two hand-holds, as if that would have saved him. He himself could not slide through the long narrow opening in the stage. He was going to be banged and shaken if the cross got free of the restraining hands, how badly he could not tell, except that a human body is frail compared to thick wood moving under its own weight.

If he escaped with broken bones he would be lucky.

5

Well, say it no more, that is twice.
The Bowyers' and Fletchers' Play

Bob Southwell arrived on the scene before
Poison was released – which showed either
how long it took to get Poison off, or how
quick Bob had been, whichever way you
liked to look at it. The fact was that he had
been on his way to the Museum Gardens to
see if all was well, and that although it
seemed like hours to the actors who were
struggling with the cross, it was only
minutes until they found a loose set of stage
steps which could be carried over and used
to stand on to untie Poison Peters.

As soon as Bob stood there looking at
them, his eyes stern behind his glasses,
everyone felt better. Authority had arrived
and authority would not let this thing
happen – and indeed a second later they
loosened the last band and Poison gingerly
moved first one arm and then the other, and
as soon as he dared, reached out a foot to
touch the steps; then he felt safer. There
were hands to hold him and support him.

At this point he released the cross of his

weight very slowly and gently, climbed down the steps in a bevy of helping hands, reached the secure stage, stood alone, and then crumpled up and fell at Bob's feet in a dead faint.

'Hospital for him,' said Bob firmly.

'He won't go in because of the fans,' explained one of the actors.

'What about the Retreat?' asked a policeman at Bob's shoulder. Grateful for the bit of local knowledge, Bob looked at him encouragingly, so the man went on.

'It's a private Quaker nursing home near the city mainly for the mentally ill, but they take other cases and they would be able to protect him from fans – I've known them have show-biz personalities before, who need a rest in private. They're very discreet.'

'Or there's the Purey Cust,' broke in another policeman. 'That's nearer.'

'Go and see what you can fix up, John,' said Bob Southwell. 'That OK by you, Mr Exelby?'

'Yes, of course. Don't worry about the fees. Anything as long as he has the chance to recover in private from this.'

'I'd be happier if he was in hospital, but...'

'He'll get good medical attention at either of those,' said someone.

While the talk was going on one of the actors had picked up Christ's garment from the ground and covered him with it.

Bob Southwell asked to see the under-stage fixing arrangements for the cross and vanished below, where he found Tom and the ASM still desperately holding the base of the cross.

'You can let that go now,' Bob said.

'Well, we know he's off, but it still might slide down.'

'I doubt if it will do any damage. Lower it.'

'Is he out of the way, up there?'

The ASM shouted up, and someone shouted down again to say that they had moved Poison and it was all right to lower the cross, no one was in the way.

Once their hands were removed, and the Soldiers up above also let go, the cross finally slipped off the scaffolding pole and thumped down so that its foot rested on the lower stage. The violent crash shocked them even though they were expecting it to happen.

'Let's have a look at this mechanism, then,' said Bob.

Tom tried not to give Bob an 'I-told-you-so' look but could only just resist reminding him that four hours before he had been ridi-culing the idea of danger. He had to close his lips firmly together and stop himself speak-ing. Even so Bob got the message. He didn't say anything but his face was grim. The twinkling humorous expression Tom liked so much had gone. The wide rounded forehead and thin lower face looked stern and concentrated.

'If it's a practical joke it's a particularly nasty one,' Bob said. 'The branch that was shoved through would hardly retain fingerprints but it's worth trying,' he remarked to one of his men, the one who had suggested the Purey Cust. 'Get someone on to it, and examine anything else that looks likely.'

He could not ignore Tom's silent questioning, and turned to him. 'Oh yes, we'll have to take action,' he said. 'Though I think this might be someone's idea of a joke. Do you have any teenagers in the cast?'

'Only the Devils – the Angels – the Virgin Mary – some of the Crowd – the Youngest Shepherd–'

'It might well be someone's idea of a funny. They might not realize the danger of real harm.'

Tom thought Bob had a touching faith in human nature, but did not like to say so in front of his men. So he smiled and nodded in agreement. The main thing was that the danger to Poison was going to be taken a bit more seriously. Two risks to Poison Peters' life – two near misses – were two too many, however caused, whether by negligence or what. The third one – and Tom was sure there was going to be a third one, didn't things always go in threes? – might succeed. Third time lucky. This time there would be nothing amateur about it.

Bob Southwell was at the police station. 'Get me Detective Chief Superintendent Duncan, please,' he said to the girl on the switchboard.

When she had rung through to Newby Wiske, got the right extension, and said, 'I have Detective Chief Inspector Southwell for you, sir,' she connected Bob with his superior.

'Good morning, sir,' said Bob. 'Yes, it's fine here. Festival weather as they keep telling me. Yes, the festival starts on Saturday. The reason I'm ringing, sir, is this: we've had two rather nasty little incidents on the set of the mystery plays. The second one last evening. How nasty? I'll tell you…'

After explaining, he went on: 'I'm inclined to think this was a practical joke that went wrong, but there have been too many unpleasant incidents connected with this production altogether. I wondered if Task Force were busy or if they could spare me a bit of manpower for supervision?… I thought they could hang around and see if there are any vandals about and try to trace the focus of trouble – it's probably in the cast… Right… Yes, sir… I'll look forward to hearing from him… Yes, the kids seem to be settling very well, thanks… Oh, fine!… I'll tell Linda, and I know she'll want me to remember her to you.'

A few minutes later his phone rang.

'Southwell.'

'You can't manage without us, then, sir? The DCS says we're to help out, pronto.'

'Diamond! You're quick off the mark.'

'Do you want us today?'

'Yes. The sooner the better. You need to get to know the set-up before this afternoon. What did the boss tell you?'

'Slight problems you can't handle, sir.'

'Get yourself down here, Sergeant Diamond, without the funny stuff, and with as many men as Task Force can spare.'

'Plain clothes?'

'Yes. How many of you will there be?'

'Ten, sir? Is that all right?'

'Yes. Fine. See you here at the station in half an hour.'

Bruce Exelby was asked to come in for consultation.

'Not before time, Mr Southwell,' he said.

'We'll have men here shortly who will spend some hours or days, or however long it takes, on duty,' replied Bob Southwell. 'I want them to mingle with your actors unobtrusively – have you any suggestions as to how we can do that?'

'We could dress them up and they could take part.'

'Have a heart, Mr Exelby, they won't have time to learn any lines.'

'They won't have lines if they are part of the Crowd.' Bruce Exelby was suddenly enthusiastic. 'They can wear costume – we made a few extra sets in case of accidental damage or other contingencies – and the Crowd is always being divided up into groups – they could be in separate groups and listen and watch. One of them could stay under the upper stage near the base of the cross to stop any more murder attempts.'

'Yes. I'd certainly thought of stationing a man there. Not that anyone is likely to try the same trick again. They would know a lookout was being kept. Murder attempts is a bit strong, Mr Exelby.'

'Murder is nearly what it was. I don't mind the people of York trying to scare Poison out of the city – I don't mind them letting off steam and all that – it's just good publicity as far as I'm concerned. What I do mind is them nearly killing him. You were there. You know how close the danger was, how delicate the business of unfastening him and getting him off the cross was. If it had crashed down with him still on it you know he would have been lucky to escape with shattered legs. What are you going to do about tracking the culprit?'

'We didn't find anything which could indicate who did it, but I suggest interviewing the younger members of the cast. To my mind this is a prank and you have quite a lot of youngsters taking part.'

'This idea of a prank is a fixation with you, Mr Southwell.' Exelby's tone was contemptuous. Bob Southwell felt like reminding him that he was a Detective Chief Inspector, not one of the cast, and was not to be spoken to in that tone of voice.

'Well, this afternoon is the photocall,' went on the director. 'The whole cast will be on set and the journalists and photographers will be having their own way. It saves a lot of trouble later. We put on whatever incident they want to photograph. They always want to do the crucifixion, from what I hear of earlier productions.'

'Peters shouldn't be expected to go through that just for the photographers.'

'No. We'll use his understudy. But I want him to do it for the last dress rehearsal, to-night. It's like driving again after an accident. The sooner the better. I want to be sure, too, that the production is right in all details because the first night is tomorrow, and once that's over I shall be leaving York and going on to my next production.'

'So soon?'

'Oh yes. I'm a busy man.'

'I somehow thought the director would be here all the time.'

'For the full three weeks? No thank you. There'd be nothing for me to do. My assistants will manage perfectly well. They can always contact me if anything comes up that really needs my attention.'

'As soon as my men arrive I'll bring them to the Museum Gardens and liaise with you there. Perhaps you'll explain what they are to do, and we'll get them fitted out with costumes. They can practise during the photocall and get used to wearing them, and begin to keep their ears open. With any luck we won't need them for long.'

Sergeant Diamond and his ten men were kitted out by Sally Vause and Velvet Smith in the parish room of St Olave. The two women were used by now to working as a team, and did the job neatly and efficiently. They did not make much impression on the men of the Task Force.

Sally was too old – and she had not aged well; her hair was dyed a suspicious shade of walnut brown, her face covered with pouches, her neck thick, and her clothes were too young for her.

Velvet at forty still had some feminine charm; the good teeth Thomas had noticed, and a brightness sometimes in her quick though subdued movements; but it was not noticeable to the men she was dressing in flowing robes. Like Tom Churchyard, they found her instantly forgettable, with her pinched figure and pale face. Only her name made any impression. Hearing Sally use it,

Sergeant Diamond asked, 'How did she get a name like that?'

Sally answered confidentially as she showed him how to tie the tapes which held the costume in place: 'Her mother was very keen on the theatre. She thought the name would look pretty in lights.'

Sergeant Diamond cast an unbelieving glance in Velvet's direction.

'Velvet was never mad on being an actress herself,' went on Sally, 'but she must have a bit of her mother's interest, or she wouldn't be working as she does towards the plays' success – you've no idea how many hours we've put in, and no one thinks of that, they just assume costumes make themselves and look after themselves.'

'I suppose she has to be thankful her mother didn't call her Satin, Muslin, or Voile,' said the Sergeant, whose wife was keen on dressmaking. 'Well, at least you're in on the action – you have the chance of watching rehearsals and all that.'

'You've got to be joking,' said Sally. 'I haven't seen a thing yet, and Velvet is never away from this place. But I'm going to watch at least some of it in rehearsal, come what may. There's that moment when God calls out to Michael – and suddenly the lights pick him out standing on that high needle of wall – I did manage to see that the other night in plain clothes and I just must see it in costume, it's so dramatic – look out for it, sergeant, don't miss it.'

'I have a job to do. We're not here to watch the plays.'

The sergeant and his men walked rather self-consciously along Almery and across Marygate and in through the St Olave's Gate, up the wooden steps and over the wall into the graveyard. Exelby met them and instantly broke up the group, heading them into different knots of players. Although the cast knew one another well there were a great many of them, and Exelby saw fit just to say things like, 'Adrian will be with you lot today,' or 'Will you have Barry in yours? You look a bit thin as you go up the stairs...'

The members of Task Force knew how to melt into backgrounds and as soon as they were with a lot of other people also dressed in medieval costume they stopped feeling self-conscious and began to do their job, chatting and mingling yet keeping their ears open and their every sense alert.

The afternoon was long and dreary. Poison Peters came on set only for a half-hour session with the photographers. He looked drawn, as if he had not slept. Thomas Churchyard got near enough to him to ask how he was, and if he had rested properly at the Retreat.

'Yeah, they were great. I'm going back

there straight after this to rest, and overnight tonight. But I want to be on my own again. I can't concentrate on preparation like I can in the caravan.' Poison's voice was low and he spoke simply to Tom. That first incident had made them friends.

'Look, if you want you could stay with me.'

'No. Thanks and all that. I *like* being on my own, particularly when there's this part to prepare for. It's like no other part on earth.'

'Will you pose with John the Baptist, Poison?' called a photographer.

Poison gave Tom an expressive look. Then he turned and in a split second had assumed the role of Christ. His movement, his whole person seemed to change, and he went towards John the Baptist as if this was a living performance.

Soon after, Exelby stopped the star's interviews and poses and sent Poison back to the Retreat in a taxi. The rest of the cast and his understudy carried on for another hour before they were allowed to go. Everyone felt exhausted. It was worse than acting.

'I'd rather be on traffic duty,' was the opinion of Sergeant Diamond.

During the afternoon one of Bob Southwell's detective inspectors was interviewing the younger members of the cast, as they were available, depending on the exigencies of the photocall. Some members of the Crowd were first. They all seemed to have stuck with their groups fairly well throughout their time on the set the previous evening. They were all at school or in work and he took notes of where they had been during the morning and afternoon for later verification.

Next the party who had been responsible for cutting the willow branches was called in. One of them admitted that on the previous day he had brought along the straight branch which had later been used to imitate an iron bolt. It had been lying on the ground among other branches torn off by a storm and he had thought it might come in useful. He had trimmed off the side branches and it had made a rather handsome stave. Claiming to have left it leaning against the back of the props tent, he was very distressed at the idea that he was implicated in the near accident.

The only other youngsters in the cast were Eve, the Virgin Mary, the Angels and the Devils. Mentally dismissing Eve and the Virgin Mary as unlikely to have had anything to do with it, Bob Southwell suggested the Angels, who were all from Queen Elizabeth's, be interviewed next, with the Devils, who were members of the Fourth Forms of the local public school, St Giles, and as full of pranks and tricks as a wagonload of monkeys.

As both Angels and Devils were under the age of seventeen, their mothers had to be present too, and this took some time and trouble to arrange.

'No, of course we aren't accusing them of anything.' Bob Southwell had to soothe a number of parents. 'Only a routine enquiry. There has been a certain amount of – horseplay, perhaps we could say...'

Velvet Smith asked to see the detective in charge of the questioning.

'It may not be relevant at all,' she said hesitantly.

'We're always pleased to hear...'

'Only that the youngsters were so long reaching the wardrobe to take off their costumes, you know, the night before this dreadful thing happened with the cross, that is, after Mr Peters had that awful accident with the electricity, that I went out to look for them, and saw one of the boys playing about with a bit of iron. It didn't look very thick, but it was metal, I'm sure, by the sound it made.'

'Thank you very much for that information.'

'It was only when I heard the pivot had been taken that I thought it might be relevant.'

'Did you see which of the boys it was?'

116

'A dark one; he had his headdress off. I said, "What are you playing about at now? Come on, all of you." So they did. I don't know what happened to the rod, or whatever it was.'

It did not take long to break down the resistance of the youngsters. Yes … they had been playing about a bit, once the performances were over… Yes, the devils had made noises to frighten the girls…

The story of the night before the accident with the cross came out.

'I hear one of the boys was trying to open one of the table tombs, and that it was your idea, is that correct?'

'Oh, how mean of him,' said the blonde Angel with brimming eyes. 'It was all his fault. I told him not to do it, I never thought he would, honestly.'

'Really, Inspector, Sergeant,' said the blonde Angel's large and formidable Mum, 'I really can't see the point of all this, my daughter would never be involved in anything…'

'It's all right. The attempt to open the tomb did not succeed, I understand. There are some scratches on the stonework, but that is not actually the matter we are investigating, and we do not hold your daughter in any way responsible.'

'I should hope not…'

'I'm only trying to get a general picture of this juvenile behaviour…'

Sure enough, one of the boys broke down under the penetrating eye of the detective inspector.

He had wanted to open the table tomb to frighten the girls … he had tried with the stick he found near the props tent but it wasn't strong enough, he wanted something which made the right kind of noise, too, he wanted to get a creaking … he had noticed the pivot bolt through the cross sticking out … Nicholas had dared him to take it … it seemed quite loose in its hole, and he decided to borrow it, just for a little while. He'd put the stick in its place so that his borrowing it wouldn't be noticed … he'd been going to put it back next day, really he had…

'Why didn't you?' asked the detective inspector, as mildly as he could make himself.

'Well,' said the Devil, with a glance at his mother, who was speechless, 'I tried to open the tomb but I couldn't. So I rattled the bolt along the railings – that was good – while we were howling…'

'And then?'

'And then I rattled it on one of those drains in the road, that was good–'

The DI was able to remember the infinite possibilities drains seemed to offer at one stage in his own life. He nodded, and waited.

'Then it sort of slipped out of my fingers and down the drain...'

'It would, wouldn't it?' said the DI.

'And I had to go to take my costume off, and then I went home. Next day I looked in our garage, and I couldn't find one like it, and I didn't dare tell anybody, and I thought the branch might be strong enough after all, and that in that case it wouldn't matter...'

Bob Southwell said nothing for a minute when told this by his DI.

Then, putting aside all the remarks about modern youth and what did parents teach their children these days which whirled through his head, he went in to speak to the boy.

The Devil – who was the largest though not the oldest of the boys – was sent home in disgrace and the school was contacted. Another member of the production was never to be allowed on the set again; they would manage with only six Devils. The headmaster agreed to have a stern word with the villain himself at once if not sooner, dwelling on such things as the honour of the school.

The police sighed breaths of relief that the act, though criminally stupid – and there was debate among the higher echelons as to whether or not the boy should be prosecuted – was at least not a deliberate attempt to injure the pop star; and for that they gave thanks.

Thomas had been told by Poison Peters that policemen were to take part in the performances; and he noticed with some amusement that although in other respects the members of Task Force looked like part of a medieval crowd, instead of sandals or bare feet they were wearing trainers, casuals, and in a few cases highly polished substantial black boots, which showed under their sweeping cloaks or tunics.

At last the final dress rehearsal had arrived. A small audience gathered in the front seats. Wives, husbands and/or parents of the performers, of the electricians, of the stage hands, of the set designer, of the ASM, and of all and sundry connected with the production, had come along.

The photocall and the police between them had thrown the whole cast into a state of the jitters. They had been told not to mention the questioning, or the two incidents which had thrown a shadow over the production.

It was a situation none of them had been in before, and combined with the awe-inspiring plays themselves and the normal tensions of a last dress rehearsal it was almost overwhelming. Most of the cast were busily doing whatever they considered calmed their nerves. Some were watching the unperturbed bowls match which was taking place on the adjoining green; some reclining on the grass of the graveyard with their backs against the stones, smoking cigarettes as if cancer had never been heard of; Humphrey Hale had made inroads already on the contents of his hip flask; Judas Iscariot was desperately peering at his copy of his lines, which had gone out of his head as completely as if an early schoolboy had taken a damp sponge and wiped clean a chalky slate.

Thomas Churchyard, the large and imperturbable, was fidgeting and wandering to and fro. He visited the dark area under the upper stage and inspected the new strong iron bolt for himself. He went up to the box from where the lights were controlled and spoke to the young man – formerly only the assistant – who had taken over the whole job. There was no longer amplification equipment on the set. He went to Poison Peters's caravan and lifted his hand to knock on the door, then changed his mind and went back via the props tent, which he looked over carefully as if it was going to sprout weapons more lethal than the hardboard spears.

At last, with the arrival of the powerful presence of Bruce Exelby from his flat in St Mary's Lodge, everything pulled together. Cigarettes were stubbed out. The hip flask disappeared into an angelic pocket. The Virgin Mary disposed of the mug of coffee she had been nervously drinking. She was standing next to the Youngest Shepherd and

121

before he left her the young man put his arm round her and gave her a hug. God stood behind a bulwark of stone next to his window arch, ready to appear for the opening words. Below him the cast moved into their various opening positions.

Some groups who had an hour to wait before they were needed went into the Tempest Anderson Hall where they could talk and play cards to while away the time, but most of the cast were too keyed up to leave the scene of the action. What untoward thing was going to happen next? What fresh danger threatened Poison Peters? As time went on and they had grown used to him, the cast had stopped thinking of him as a pop star and begun to think of him in his new persona; he was central to their play. He was like the boss of stamens in a rose; they the petals surrounding him, he the embodiment of Christ.

And it went beautifully.

Poison Peters performed as if lifted out of himself – as if this was not Poison Peters the revolting pop star but Christ as he might have been, combining intense humility with dignity and power. The watchers forgot everything else but the mystery plays. The members of the Task Force found themselves caught up in acting out the most vital of all the experiences of mankind. They lived through the story as if it was new to them, as if it was happening at that very moment in time. Against the sky God looked down and was moved by the plight of His people and His Son beneath him.

When the crucifixion approached Thomas Churchyard exercised his prerogative of leaving his throne, which he had been using for some scenes. It was a strain to sit up there, and not necessary again until the Taylors' Play, but he thought he would go up for the start of the Saddlers' Play, the Harrowing of Hell.

He didn't think he could sit above while Poison went through the mental agony of being lifted by the pivoting cross in the Pinners' and Painters' Play, remembering with him the scene of the previous day. Neither did he want to sit up there during the long minutes of Poison's physical and mental anguish during the Butchers' Play. For, with everything that could be done to alleviate it, anguish if not in truth agony it was and must be, to be endured nightly, solitary yet in front of all.

Once Poison was lifted down, then Thomas felt he himself would be able to relax and take part in things again. So while the agony was going on Thomas sat on the wooden walkway along the scaffolding and listened, out of sight behind the abbey masonry.

It was over, and Christ had been taken down from the cross and placed in the tomb. Whatever Poison had thought and felt, Thomas could tell from what he had heard and from the general atmosphere, that Poison had acted supremely well. Thomas himself was shaking. In relief, he thought. The worst was over now.

And sure enough, a minute later Poison came climbing up the ladder to the walkway, freshly dressed in a white robe, and sat down near him out of sight of the stage. 'All right?' asked Tom. Poison nodded. Then he huddled himself within the robe and bent his head, with a gesture of one hand which said plainer than words, 'I'm all right but I want to be left alone.' There would be ten minutes or so rest for him before he had to make his blinding appearance in the archway next to them and confound Lucifer and all his works.

Straightening up, Thomas decided to climb the ladder to his platform and throne. Before doing so he took a leisurely survey of the scene below him. Evening was deepening into night. The lights on the set seemed to make the sky black by contrast. In the distance the bowls players had packed up and gone home, and their green looked grey in the deep shadows. Nearer at hand he had the peaceful scene of the graveyard of St Olave's, and the lovely ancient church of St

Olaf himself, both lit by stray beams of light, to look at. It always amused him to see the cast waiting among the gravestones. Now they were silent, listening intently to the play so that they could move into position in good time for their next entrance. They might indeed have been ghosts, medieval ghosts in the graveyard.

Here and there he recognized friends. There was Judas Iscariot, talking to the other Apostles. Then Peter, Thomas, John and James went off, presumably to be ready for the Scriveners' Play, though it was not for a while yet. Judas was left alone and wandered over to talk to a group of the Crowd. The woman who carried a spindle was actually spinning from it, even in the gathering dark, and winding the wool on, in between creating the thread. For centuries women must have used every spare second like that. Glancing down at his feet Thomas saw the shadowy form of one of the Devils running, hips swivelling, towards the east end of the Abbey where the others must be waiting for the cue for their entrance in the Harrowing of Hell.

Everyone was going to be needed at the end for the great crowd scene in the Mercers' Play, the Day of Judgement. Then the Good Souls would mount the steps to the window openings, and line up behind them on the wooden walk along the scaffolding, looking down from their blessed state on to the scene of the Bad Souls being thrown down the long slope to the flames of Hell's Mouth, with Lucifer and the Devils standing by to harry them on their way.

Thomas turned reluctantly and climbed his ladder. He stepped slowly – the drop on to the stage looked like an abyss – in front of the throne, and lowered himself on to it. Once here he had to be careful. He was in view, and must behave like God and not like Thomas Churchyard, telecommunications engineer. All the same, he could move his eyes, and thought it was permissible to incline his head gently as if looking down with interest and compassion on his creatures.

The scene below him was Hell. It was the Saddlers' Play, the Harrowing of Hell. Adam and Eve were sitting in the centre of the lower stage, and Adam was speaking. Isaiah walked across and stood near to them, ready to chime in with his speech. Presently John the Baptist and then Moyses would make their appearance, before the Devils joined the scene.

The set was complex, with two main levels, but with wide staircases joining them and slopes up and down, and it was working very well. It looked so like the ancient stone which backed it that many people were deceived into thinking that ruins and set were all one, all weather-worn limestone, and did not realize that so much of what they saw was wood covered by painted expanded polystyrene.

Directly below Thomas was the cross, now empty, the upper stage on which it was fixed almost level with the bottom of the window archways. In front of it a flight of stairs led down to the flat lower stage where Adam and Eve were sitting and where Isaiah stood. On the left was the long slope downward with its flanking low wall, behind which and out of sight of the audience a narrow ladder led down to the under-stage area. On the right was the flight of steps up to another window, where later the saved souls would climb to Heaven. Further still to the right was the broad stairway leading down under the stage.

Thomas could see the three wide stairways which led down to ground level, but he could not see the lower exits and entrances because of the jut of the wide stage. It was all very familiar to him by now; 'like the back of my hand,' he thought and smiled. Did one really know the back of one's hand? Seeing it among a thousand others would one pick it out through its distinctive bumps and hollows? Then he remembered that God, watching his creatures in Hell, would not smile, and he smoothed out his features. Yet he could not resist taking a look down sideways at the back of his left hand, as it lay calmly on the arm of the throne. His glance passed on below.

A figure was climbing slowly up the narrow ladder behind the long slope. It was the flicker of movement in an unexpected place that caught Thomas's attention. He inclined his head a little more, slowly and graciously. A black curly head was rising into the broad light of the set. Bruce Exelby. Now what was the matter? Trust him to go interrupting the scene just when it was going so well.

Exelby's hand clutched the wide wall between the ladder and the slope and he came gradually into full view. He heaved himself up on to the stage, walked forward, and stood there swaying slightly. Adam had faltered in his speech and fallen silent, looking apprehensive.

Above, it was so quiet that Thomas could hear Exelby's heavy breathing, and the thought flashed through his head that the director must be very out of condition to be winded by the short climb up the ladder. But the loud breathing died away, seemed to become quicker and quieter as the director stumbled forward. He reeled almost into Isaiah, then wavered a couple of steps farther, before collapsing altogether and lying face down.

Red-stained bubbles foamed from his

mouth and tinted the dusty dun of the boards of the stage a gentle pink. One of his hands reached forward in front of his head towards the drop on to ground level, touching and almost caressing the edge of the wood.

Sergeant Diamond, dressed in plain clothes, had been sitting with the other people in the audience. He jumped to his feet and ran forward up the flight of steps nearest to him on to the stage level where the action had been taking place, before Thomas had had time to do more than take in that something was very wrong.

Bending over the director, the sergeant took hold of his wrist and felt for his pulse. Straightening, he yelled at Isaiah, 'See if there's a doctor here!' and turning round in a circle, shouted to all and sundry, 'The performance is suspended. Mr Exelby is ill. Clear the stage please. Tell my men to come here.'

Adam and Eve, John the Baptist, Moyses, the little Devils, Belzebub, and Satan, who had all been either on stage or waiting in the wings, obeyed him and made a group on the grass at the front of the seats. Isaiah had gone rushing to find a telephone.

One of Task Force came running from the graveyard and up on to the stage.

Sergeant Diamond was holding Exelby's wrist in one hand and the radio in the other, speaking rapidly to the station. 'Emergency at the mystery plays site, Museum Gardens,' he said. 'Director taken ill. Get an ambulance here. Pulse rapid and weak. Unconscious.' He looked up at his man. 'Get that lot out of here,' with a glance at the spectators.

The man from Task Force gathered up his skirts and left the stage. First he spoke to the audience. 'Would you all go home, please? There will be nothing else to watch tonight.' Then to the group of actors, 'The rehearsal won't go on. Would you change out of costume, please. You schoolboys can go home.'

'Can we all go home?' asked Eve.

'You can, miss.'

'I want to know how he is and what's happening,' said Adam.

'Then perhaps you'd wait after changing.'

The actors went off silently, glancing backward. Even the little Devils seemed subdued as they scampered into the darkness. More Task Force men had arrived and the first one had put them rapidly in the picture. They went back to the rest of the cast to tell them to get out of costume, the play was over. Thomas had come down from his pinnacle and with everyone else trooped off to change. In passing he had spoken briefly to Poison.

'What now?' the singer had asked, lifting his head.

'Exelby is ill. Some sort of collapse.'

Poison had sighed. 'That puts the tin lid on it. There's a jinx on this thing.'

'Come on. Go to the caravan and have a cup of tea.'

Poison had unfolded himself and followed Tom down the scaffolding, drooping wearily and shivering.

'There blows a cold wind today, today,/ The wind blows cold today...' he murmured as if saying goodbye to Tom. As Tom watched him walk off into the night he thought what a difference adrenalin makes. If he had been going on stage now the man would have been radiant with energy. And in his mind he completed the quotation: 'Christ suffered His passion for mannes salvation. To keep the cold wind away.' The cold wind was blowing with a vengeance.

Getting down from the scaffolding had delayed Thomas and Poison. The others were already walking either towards the Tempest Anderson Hall or through the St Olave's Gate. Poison had vanished in the direction of the caravan as Tom rounded the edge of the masonry, supposedly on his way to the Tempest Anderson Hall, and came briefly in sight of the front of the stage. He knew gawpers were the last thing needed but he could not resist a quick look at the stage where Exelby lay still and Sergeant Diamond knelt beside him. Then the sergeant lifted his head and stood up. In the distance the scream of an approaching ambulance could be heard. The sergeant spoke to one of Task Force.

'I think he's dead.'

By Sergeant Diamond's watch he had been kneeling by Bruce Exelby for exactly two minutes.

6

Make ready, and ding you him down,
And deafen us no more with his deeds.
                        The Bowyers' and Fletchers' Play

DCI Southwell got the message at home. He
had been thinking about Task Force and
wondering whether to go down to the
Museum Gardens to see how they were getting on, but he was not prepared for Sergeant
Diamond's urgent voice.

'We've had a death, sir. The DI is on his
way but asked me to speak directly to you.'

'Poison Peters?' asked Bob.

'No, sir. The director, Mr Exelby.'

'What the heck... How? Where?'

'How – we don't know the cause yet. Could
be natural, I suppose, but I don't think so, sir.
He had bloody foam coming from his mouth
and there's quite a lot of blood now. We're
just waiting for a doctor to confirm death but
I've no doubt of it. Where – he died at my
feet, sir. On the stage.'

'Witnesses?'

'Too many if anything.'

'Hold everyone. Don't let them go home.
The best place for them would be the

133

Tempest Anderson Hall, I think. I'm on my way.'

The sergeant coughed. 'Some of them have already gone, sir.'

Bob Southwell swore picturesquely and slammed down the handset.

Detective Inspector Smart had already arrived on the scene when Bob Southwell got there. He had coincided with the ambulance and the doctor. The doctor had knelt beside Exelby, taking Sergeant Diamond's place, and examined the body. The sergeant explained things rapidly to his superior.

The doctor was about to flip Bruce Exelby onto his back. He had reached forward to take a grip of the shoulder. He lifted him slightly. Then he paused, looking up at DI Smart, and by a glance indicated a small area of blood, hardly more than a spot, dark crimson, on the left side of Exelby's shirt towards the front.

Letting go, the doctor allowed the body to slump forward once more.

'It's pretty obvious he's dead,' he remarked. 'And that looks like a wound to me. I don't think I ought to disturb him further. You are going to want to investigate.'

'You can certify he's dead?'

'Yes.'

'We'll have to treat this as a suspicious death then. Possible murder.'

'You'll only know exactly with a post-mortem.'

The blood had been flowing freely from Exelby's mouth and nose. The pool on the boards was no longer that delicate pink of the first touch.

'Diamond, please ask for the scene-of-crime officers to be sent down here. Get someone appointed as coroner's officer and see they send a message to the coroner. There are still a lot of people about. Perhaps you'd better ask for screens and get them put round the body. Tape a path to the body for everyone to use, we don't want any more disturbance of the forensic evidence than we've had already.'

Bob Southwell drove in through the gates of the Museum Gardens. The man on duty at the gates was one of the constables from Task Force. Bob's headlights lit up the curving gravel footpath before him, cutting a swathe of light through black trees and bushes. He drove unceremoniously. The dark back of the grandstand was pierced by cracks of light, the grass and gravel cut up by the wheels of police car and ambulance. Above, the stage lighting irradiated the sky; the arches were glowing white gold; the more distant sky a black backdrop behind them.

As Bob arrived the van from the station

came up behind him, and as he reached the stage and stood beside the body of Bruce Exelby, the two constables with the screens were already lifting them from the van and carrying them through the gateway and up the flight of stairs.

It had only been that morning that Exelby had been making a nuisance of himself in the police station, demanding action. Bob could not help thinking that it looked as though his demands had been justified. The big body still looked strong and fit in death. The hair curled as crisply. What could be seen of the face held no look of pain. It had been smoothed out, emptied.

'Is that the way he was?' Bob asked the doctor.

'Yes. I haven't moved him. Well, perhaps a fraction as I was examining him, but it was obvious at first that he must be dead, so I didn't turn him over. I lifted him slightly and then let him drop back again.'

'That's all right, then. We want to know because of the photographs.'

'I don't think we need detain you and the ambulance any further,' the DI said to the doctor. 'We'll almost certainly be calling the Home Office pathologist and a team from the forensic science lab to take tests. Perhaps we can call on you later to give a statement when you are off duty.'

Sergeant Diamond had been busy again

with his radio.

The photographers arrived and began to use up several rolls of film.

The pathologist and the forensic scientist arrived, and so did an undertaker. As he was a local man, he looked around for someone to talk to, and could only find the members of Task Force. A few at a time they had gone to change out of their costumes, and one of them, now dressed in jeans and anorak, told him a little of what had been happening. The undertaker's habitual look of discretion hid fervent curiosity. There was no way he was going to betray his interest, but this was the vindication of all that the people of the city had thought. The director, responsible for the pollution of the mystery plays by Poison Peters, had been punished. To the undertaker it seemed as if heaven itself had had a hand in the matter.

The pathologist and the forensic scientist seemed to spend a long time standing at a distance with their hands in their pockets, just looking at Exelby, at the place he was lying, and taking in the surroundings.

Then they moved in on the body. They had worked together before and for anyone who knew what they were watching it was a beautiful bit of teamwork, like a *pas de deux* in a ballet. They exchanged a few words in undertones. Their movements were small-scale but neat and swift. After a few minutes

137

they lifted the shirt and confirmed the thought of the doctor – there was a wound in the left chest, a hardly visible puncture, which had only oozed a little blood. They slid plastic bags over Exelby's head, hands and feet. The crisp curls were crushed down by the translucent film, the hands which had made so many arrogant gestures looking strangely blundering. The two men wrapped Exelby's whole body in a corpse-sheet of plastic. At this point the undertaker went back to his van, and with his assistant, who had been waiting in the passenger seat and listening to his Walkman, brought the undertaker's shell, and soon was lifting the director into it and carrying him off the stage which had been his kingdom.

The forensic scientist, whose name was Brian and who had had to leave a wife, kids, and a perfectly good television programme to come down here, took a quick look around.

'He came up those steps at the back,' said Sergeant Diamond, showing him. They went down together. The steps were hardly more than a ladder and narrow for Diamond. Under the stage it was completely dark, but Brian had a powerful torch, and by its light looked intently at every step, then swung the beam on to the grass. Sergeant Diamond knew what was being looked for: blood, drops, splashes, signs of struggle. He felt like saying that there wouldn't be any drops or splashes – that he himself had seen the first blood rise to Exelby's lips, in that dreadful pink foam, as he stumbled across the stage – but he said nothing. In this area the grass had been constantly trampled over the last days as the actors made their way from one part of the set to another, out of sight of the stands.

They went to the entrance through the ancient walls into the graveyard of St Olave's, without seeing anything which seemed significant.

'Have to look with floodlighting,' said Brian as they prepared to go back up the ladder. 'Hopeless now. See if you can get some rigged up before I get back from the mortuary. No trampling about though. You'll be seeing no one comes in here until I've done a proper examination.'

'Yes, sir.'

'Better go to the mortuary, I suppose.'

The pathologist was waiting for him. Bob Southwell was walking back from the Tempest Anderson Hall, and decided to go with them. They set off together, following the undertaker's van.

Earlier, once the pathologist and forensic scientist had arrived, Bob had left the set and gone to the Tempest Anderson Hall, where the actors, subdued, had been waiting for him. Some of course had gone home in the first few minutes after the announcement that Exelby was ill. The others had changed out of their costumes, and were waiting uneasily, not knowing what was happening and what to expect.

Time had dragged; many of them had wondered whether to go home or not. Thomas, from overhearing Sergeant Diamond, knew that the director was dead, but he told no one. Afterwards he wondered why he had said nothing, and decided that it was because he could hardly believe it himself. He could not take in that such a thing could happen so quickly and so mysteriously.

There was talk, of course; general gossip about how things were going, worries about the city's reaction to Poison Peters – most of the cast had stopped resenting him and were now only anxious for the success of the plays; worries about what was wrong with Bruce Exelby; speculation about whether he had recovered consciousness yet, and about the cause of his sudden collapse.

There was a stir among them as though a giant spoon had agitated the air in the hall when Bob Southwell walked through the door, between the two Task Force men. He walked in with that air of authority which is unmistakeable.

Bob had moved on to the platform; whether it was his presence, or the news he had to tell, Thomas could not decide, but they were all in the hollow of the hand of this tall slim man with the large glasses.

He spoke without beating about the bush, without any preliminaries.

'I am very sorry to have to tell you that your director, Mr Bruce Exelby, has died.' There was a stunned murmur during Bob's pause. 'We are unfortunately having to treat the death as suspicious, and we would like to talk to each of you and try to piece together the events of the evening.'

He paused again; this time a profound silence filled the gap.

'We will be setting up an incident room and would like to see you all there individually tomorrow; it will probably be here in the Museum Gardens. Now, we would like all your names and addresses, if you will give them as you go out.'

Everyone seemed to draw breath into their lungs at once. Bob had spoken very slowly, so that every word had time to sink in. Humphrey Hale was the first to gather his wits.

'You tell us he has died,' he said. 'Can you tell us how this had come about?'

Bob answered carefully. 'You are all aware that Mr Exelby collapsed on stage. At that point you were asked to leave the area while efforts were being made to help him. In fact he died. There are indications that there is

141

something suspicious about this unexpected death. We will be making routine inquiries. At the moment we cannot tell you what caused the death, but you will be kept informed. The questions will be normal police procedure in a case like this.'

It appeared as though Bob might have nothing else to say, so Thomas Churchyard got up hastily, with a half-smile and gesture to him, and turned to the cast.

'I'm sure you agree with me, ladies and gentlemen, that we must not let this affect the mystery plays. That is the last thing Bruce Exelby would have wanted. This production is his creation and we owe it to him to give it all we've got and make it the best performance ever, even if he isn't here to get on to our bones and make us do well.'

'The play must go on,' said Lucifer.

'That's right. So are we agreed on that?'

There was a gentle sound of assent.

'Sue,' said Tom, turning to Sue Brown the assistant director, who was sitting among the actors. 'You'll have to take charge.'

She stood up, white-faced. 'Yes, you're right of course, Tom. Everyone – business as usual. The first performance is always the most trying and goodness knows how we're going to get through, but for everybody's sake, including all the people who'll be coming to see us, we've got to. Try to rest well tonight even if you can't sleep. The arrange-

142

ments already made for tomorrow stand. Now perhaps, since the police say we can go, we should all get home.'

Bob nodded assent. The two detectives were at each side of the door with notebooks. Everyone got up and began crowding towards them, talking furiously. Over the heads of the others Tom's eyes met Bob's and he was given a friendly wave. 'See you later,' said Bob's lips soundlessly. Tom felt himself relax. It looked as though he himself was not regarded with suspicion, which was a relief. It would have been very uncomfortable living next to Bob and Linda if he was regarded as a potential ... murderer?

For a moment Thomas's mind went blank. Suspicious death, they had said. No word of murder. But he knew instinctively that that was what it must be. It could hardly be a heart attack, with that bloody foam issuing from nose and mouth – he had been near enough to see it, on his walk to the Tempest Anderson Hall. Exelby had always seemed very fit. He couldn't have had an accident, surely? How? Under the stage? No, it must be – if 'suspicious' – it must be murder.

And if Bob had signalled to him, 'See you later,' and Tom had not misread his lips, then he himself was not under suspicion. Though surely everyone must be equally suspect? Then he realized anew what he had been thinking. Murder, the killing of one

143

human being by another ... someone on the set tonight must have done it. He shivered.

It was then that he realized Poison was not with them in the Hall. He went over to Bob Southwell and said: 'Poison Peters isn't here, he won't know. Is it all right if I go to his caravan and tell him?'

'I'll come with you.'

Once the press of actors at the door had lessened, Bob and Tom went together the few yards to the silver-grey caravan its wide streak of shining silver catching the reflected gleams from the stage lighting. Poison opened the door to them reluctantly. 'Oh, it's you,' he said to Tom.

'Detective Chief Inspector Southwell,' Tom introduced Bob. 'Can we come in?'

'I don't like the look of your arriving here in tandem like this,' said Poison. 'What's been happening? Whenever I get the police to see me they're hunting for drugs, yeah?'

'Not to worry, Mr Peters,' said Bob. 'May we come in?'

Poison let them in, but only just, Tom felt. 'Any tea going?' he asked to break the atmosphere. 'We could use a cup.'

Poison was still quiet and suspicious, but he filled the kettle without comment, gestured them to a seat, and set out fluted cups and saucers on the flap table. Tom felt that Bob must be taking everything in, but the policeman's manner was calm and easy

144

and betrayed no surprise when he was handed a cup of clear weak Earl Grey tea in delicate china.

'I'm ready for this,' he remarked.

Poison made no move to take his own, but sat facing them and waiting to hear what they had to say. When the words came – however gently put – it could be seen that they were a shock to him, although he barely moved a muscle. At last he said in a forced tone to Tom, 'Told you there was a jinx on this thing, yeah?'

'Performance goes on as usual tomorrow.' Tom's deep voice came comfortingly, reassuringly normal. 'Sue Brown will be in charge.'

'Good girl,' said Poison. At last he picked up his cup. As if to reinforce to Bob an impression of loutishness, to counteract the tea and the almost dainty general aspect of the caravan, he slurped at it loudly. As soon as they had all finished their cupfuls, he rose and said, 'Well, be seeing ya, yeah?' and Bob and Tom gracefully went.

'I'll go home if that's all right,' said Tom when they were outside the caravan. 'See you when you interview me tomorrow.'

'Don't worry too much,' said Bob.

'You mean I'm not under suspicion?'

'It looks as if you were sitting enthroned in the sky when the deed must have been done.'

'But you don't know.'

145

'No. And for heaven's sake don't quote me in case you have done it after all,' said Bob in a light manner.

'My God … you really think it's murder…'

There was a silence for a few seconds. The two men looked at one another in the odd mixture of light and darkness. The electrician up in the lighting box at the top of the stand of seats had been relieved long ago by a detective who knew enough about lighting to be responsible for running it for as long as it was needed. Apart from this the night had deepened. The golden halo of threads of light over the city could be seen faintly, high over their heads.

Then Bob went to join the pathologist and the forensic scientist and Tom went in search of his bicycle.

'I think we're due for a beer,' said the pathologist, straightening his back.

Forensics looked at his watch. 'Just time before they shut,' he remarked.

'I can do with one,' added Bob Southwell.

He hadn't enjoyed the past half hour or so in the mortuary. These chaps obviously did enjoy the grisly job in a kind of way; dead bodies they were used to; it was the excitement of discovery, detection, which fascinated them. Clothing bagged individually. More photographs. Wound traced to make a 'guesstimate' of size, depth, and direction of weapon. Collect blood, urine, etc. Carry out rest of PM to exclude natural causes. He had hated being there while they did it.

Seeming to divine his thoughts the pathologist said, 'This was a nice one, you know, compared to most. If they've been dead a long time even we find it pretty stomach-turning.'

'Let's have that beer,' replied Bob, and it wasn't until they were in the Angler's Arms, with its curious internal courtyard overlooked on all sides by upper-floor windows, that they went back to the subject. The pub was quiet that night apart from a group of Dutch teenage tourists filling the small bar area. The three men got a corner by the fireplace in one of the small rooms, and although it was too warm for the delights of glowing coals, the shaded lights rid them of the harsh glare of the mortuary and the beer took some of the taste of death out of their mouths.

'Bring us good ale, and bring us good ale / For our Blessed Lady's sake, bring us good ale,' said Brian.

'You've been watching too many mystery plays,' said Bob; then, 'Well?' to the pathologist. There was no one likely to overhear.

'I'll go straight home and type out my report for the coroner.'

'Have a heart! I need to know something now.'

'Right. Just for you.' The pathologist found a notepad in his pocket and began to cover it with his near-indecipherable writing, talking as he did so. 'One blow. A knife of the stiletto type, narrow-bladed. He was stabbed on the level of the nipple on his left side, slightly to the rear. This punctured the aorta and pulmonary artery, small punctures.'

'How long before he died do you think he was knifed?'

'I would guess he would lose consciousness in about forty seconds after the blow, and die in two or not more than three minutes. I *would* have said two, but you told me, Bob, that Sergeant Diamond was standing by him for two minutes, and before that Exelby'd climbed that narrow stair on to the stage. I would guess that he'd been attacked only seconds before that.'

'So it had to be someone in the cast. I think we can exempt Task Force. The audience couldn't have done it either.'

'Surely anyone could have wandered on to the set? Incidentally, there's going to be no help from forensics.'

'Why not?'

Brian was lugubrious. 'He didn't bleed immediately. Therefore, no blood on the culprit. Well – let's qualify that. There might have been the slightest trace on the hand of the assassin, from withdrawing the knife, but it would be very slight indeed; the blood from the wound was very little altogether – the stain on the shirt only an inch across, even after death. The victim seems to have been taken by surprise – there's nothing under his fingernails, for instance; he doesn't seem to have gone for his attacker. I wouldn't mind betting in fact that he never knew what happened.'

'How can you be murdered and not know what's happened?'

'Easily. Someone's coming past – stops to speak to you – makes a lunge at you with a thin knife – you might think at first they've just given you a friendly poke in the ribs, a bit overdone it, perhaps.'

'Oh, come on, Brian,' said the pathologist. 'There'd be a searing pain, surely.'

'There aren't many nerve endings once you've got in through the skin.'

'True. I still think it would feel like a kick in the ribs from a wild horse.'

'You wouldn't necessarily realize you'd been knifed.'

'No, you might not.'

'Then his breathing starts getting difficult; he realizes something is wrong. Wanting to get help he climbs the ladder on to the stage. By now the internal bleeding is really getting under way. He feels dizzy, tries to speak, can't do that. Feels faint. Loses consciousness. Blood coming up in throat. End of stout party.'

Bob drank the last of his beer and tried to erase the picture from his mind. Taking the scribbled notes from the pathologist, he said something about going and got to his feet. 'Give you a lift?' he asked Forensics.

'I think I'd like to walk back. By the time we reach your car and drive there I could have been working ten minutes.'

'Goodnight, then.'

'Are you ringing the detective chief superintendent?' asked Brian.

'Wait till this gets in the papers,' said the pathologist.

Bob Southwell rang Detective Chief Superintendent Duncan from Ouse Avenue. Linda had called downstairs sleepily when he came in. There was no sound from the children. He thought of Thomas Churchyard next door, no doubt also asleep by now. Sitting down in a chair for a moment, Bob almost dropped off himself. To bring his alertness back he went and made himself a powdered coffee and hoped it wouldn't keep him awake all night. Then at last, with a nervous look at the clock, he walked over to the telephone.

'Sorry to disturb you, sir. I hope you weren't asleep.'

'It's quite all right, Southwell,' but the words came over the line one at a time, like small but weighty blocks of ice.

Bob explained briefly.

'My God, the papers will get hold of this.'

'I'm afraid they will.'

'And the radio. And the television. We'll have the whole of the blasted media down on us, Bob.'

'I'll have to tell the assistant chief constable, better ring him now. He won't be very pleased at being disturbed.'

'No, sir.'

'I'd better come down myself tomorrow – organize a press conference, that kind of thing. Perhaps the assistant chief would speak to the press. He's bound to be very concerned. I'll see what he thinks. Leave that to me, Southwell.'

'I wish we could keep it under wraps for a bit. Give us more chance of finding the bastard who's done it.'

'Don't we all! How much easier it would be without blasted reporters! But that's life, Southwell. Ten to one there's been a leak already. In a place like York, and a lot of people involved – how many in the cast alone?' But he did not wait for an answer. 'It'll get out – bound to. You might not have long. Hours, perhaps, before the whole lot are round your neck.'

'We'd better announce it straight away.'

'The morning will be soon enough. Say ten o'clock for the press conference and official announcement. I'll come to see you first thing. Got everything under control?'

'Yes, sir.'

Bob set his alarm for half past five.

Brian, the forensic scientist, had found nothing, although he had been searching carefully with another of his team for half an hour. The area under the stage was not un-pleasant in the still watches of the night.

At last, a portable floodlight in his hand, crawling across the crushed grass on all fours with his nose an inch from the ground, Brian happened to glance sideways; a glint of something under one of the supports caught his eye. He went over at once, and got down again to peer under the horizontal beam of wood. The knife did not look as though it had been deliberately pushed underneath; it looked as though, casually hurled away, it had fallen flat and bounced sideways, as Brian had noticed knives sometimes did when dropped on the kitchen floor, and so hidden itself under the wooden framework. He found a penknife in his pocket and poked delicately, moving one end of the knife out from its hiding place until at last he was able to pick it up with wrapped fingers and drop it into a plastic bag.

His team-mate let out a long gasp of breath.

'I think we'll go home now.' There was undeniable pride in Brian's voice.

'That really looks like a murder weapon,' whispered the other.

'Meant for him, must have been. Even got his initials on it,' said Brian, showing the handle, with two letters inlaid in silver dots: B.E.

7

Haha! This was a merry note,
By the death that I shall die,
I have so croaked in my throat
That my lips are near dry.
            The Chaundlers' Play

The dawn of the first day of the festival
spread over the city. It was going to be fine
and warm – festival weather. The visitors
from all over the world were not yet stirring
in their beds, the buskers had not yet even
thought about taking their varied instruments out into the streets and beginning to
spread their web of sound. The sunbeams
licked awake the sparkles of gilt embellish-
ing black wrought iron and carven heraldry;
the spires and towers of the ancient
churches shone cream and rose in the first
light. The spire of All Saints North Street in
particular was in such a rose glow that the
stone seemed incandescent pink. The east
end of the Minster glittered dazzling gold,
its vast tennis court of a window reflecting
ten thousand facets of sunlight.

The incident post had already been set up
in the form of a second caravan in the

Museum Gardens, for the police force rests not neither does it sleep. The murder room was in the police station itself. Teams of men were being drafted in from North Yorkshire, and eventually gathered fifty strong to set up the murder system, to find and sift information. A computer, its blank, powerful memory ready to be imprinted, was waiting.

At half past seven, when Thomas Churchyard arrived at his office to collect some papers, Bob Southwell had already been in the incident post for over an hour.

'We don't want to disturb the performance at all,' Bob had said. 'So if you forensic people can possibly be finished by then. We really ought to get someone to clean the stage. It's going to be bad enough for them without having to act round the blood.'

There were hundreds of people to interview. A master list was being compiled, teams were being made up, and each man was given his own list of people to see and a number of standard questions. The results would then be fed into the computer. Meanwhile the most obviously important witnesses were going to come one by one into the incident post to see the detectives who would be working there.

Bob Southwell was not meant to be actively investigating in this first stage; he had enough to do seeing that all wheels were set in motion and preparations made for the descent of the assistant chief constable and Detective Chief Superintendent Duncan later in the day. He did not expect them until late morning, by which time he hoped to have the initial work under way. A press-relations man arrived from HQ to liaise with him and organize contacts with the media, and he had to be shown the local ropes before he could be of real use.

Thomas did not usually work on a Saturday, and had officially begun his leave, but a manhole was being enlarged in the middle of one of the narrow medieval streets – the worst possible time of year to carry out such work from a traffic-flow point of view – they would not have done it if an emergency had not arisen. He felt compelled to make sure all was going as smoothly as possible. The contractors were already busy, having, like the police, worked through half the night. Traffic cones, shortly to be knocked over, defined a narrower than ever passage for the cars of residents and visitors alike. Emergency traffic lights were installed and in operation. Tom's second in command was there, looking competent, calm and in control.

Leaving the scene with his conscience a little clearer Tom walked towards the Museum Gardens. Both he and Bob were to meet a pretty girl that morning, and Tom's was walking towards him now.

She looked breathless and helpless, a lot of white-blonde hair framing a lovely face with wide blue eyes; she wore a fawn raincoat belted over an hourglass figure.

'Which is ze way to ze railway station?' she asked, looking at Thomas as though her life depended on his reply. He explained carefully, remembering a film he had once seen starring Mai Zetterling. She listened, but the minute he stopped speaking she asked, 'Which is ze way to ze Castle Museum?' So he explained again, then turned to watch her go, thinking that the way she was taking wouldn't lead her to either of them.

Bob's encounter was less light-hearted. He had to meet Bruce Exelby's secretary at the station.

She was a tall girl, self-possessed and beautiful.

'But why should anyone murder Bruce?' she asked. 'Was it in mistake for Poison Peters?'

'That's a possibility.' Not really though, thought Bob. Not in mistake for. Because of, perhaps.

'I suppose it's that Absolom man. He must be a bit unhinged.'

'What do you know about that?'

'Bruce told me on the phone. He was just about steaming.'

'As far as we know Absolom had nothing

to do with it.'

Zita was in York to do two things; to make funeral arrangements and to clear the flat, taking Exelby's possessions back with her. The police had already gone through the flat in case there was anything helpful, but Exelby had brought very few things with him and nothing was added to their knowledge.

With the aid of a nice young constable Zita soon packed the clothes into suitcases and papers into a briefcase. The constable, who had been told to help as much as he could, took the cases down to the station while Bob took Zita to make the funeral arrangements. He went with her to the door of the mortuary and watched as she walked forward to the body and stood motionless looking down at the still face. He went out to the car and sat waiting for her.

She was calm, almost rigid in feature, when she came and got in beside him.

'It *was* Absolom, then,' she said bitterly. 'And because of that crackpot I've lost a perfectly good job.'

Bob whipped his head around to look at her. She needed no encouragement to go on. 'The undertaker told me. He talked to the stage electrician last night, who told him there'd been the father and mother of a row. Absolom had been warned off the place, but he was in the audience at the dress rehearsal and Bruce went absolutely mad.'

'And?' asked Bob.

'And the man went off, but obviously he just concealed himself and waited till he could have a go at Bruce.'

'I'll look into it.' Bob drove her to the station. As they drew up there he decided to do one more thing. He produced the stiletto knife, in its polythene bag. Forensics had already gone over it, and he was taking it to the murder room to be exhibit A. 'Could you just look at this for me? Can you identify it as Exelby's?'

Zita shuddered and refused to take it in her hands. Bob turned it over and round and round for her.

'I've never seen it before in my life.'

'You've never seen it?' But these initials on the end – B.E. Perhaps he had it in a drawer or tucked away somewhere at his flat.'

'Look. He worked a lot from home. I was in his flat all the time. What's more I packed his things for him when he came up here – he had an appointment and was going to be rushed. No, I wasn't his mistress if that's what you're thinking. Not that he didn't try it on. But I've a perfectly good boyfriend and we're saving to get married... Yes, he must have had things packed away I never saw. I saw all the things he brought with him though, and he was wearing those skin-tight jeans and a T-shirt when he left. If he'd had a thread underneath it would have showed,

160

so he hadn't got a knife stuck in his belt. Why does it have to be his just because it's got B.E. on it? Could be anybody's.'

Bob had no reason to disbelieve her. He put exhibit A away and politely got out of the car and opened the passenger door. The young police constable came forward, carrying the suitcases. She smiled around graciously and departed.

She had made the arrangements with the undertaker. The police had no objection to the funeral taking place as soon as the inquest was over. There was nothing else to learn from the body. Exelby had no near relatives; Zita was acting on behalf of the lawyer who had been Exelby's friend, and was now his executor. 'It gives me a few days more work, tidying up,' she had said. 'Then it'll be back to the agency. Just when I thought that if I played my cards right I'd have a job for as long as I wanted it.'

As Bob parked his car beside the police caravan he saw Thomas Churchyard approaching. He decided to leave the matter of the undertaker's evidence and the row with Absolom for the moment. He attracted Thomas's attention and said, 'Just the man I want.'

'I'm not sure that I like the sound of that.'

'You're here early! The performance isn't until tonight, is it?'

'Half past seven. Finishes about half past

161

eleven or a quarter to twelve.'

'Bit gruelling, surely? Every day for three weeks on top of working for a living?'

'Well, I'm taking annual leave this year. But a lot of people do work and take part as well, that's right. It is exhausting. But there's a group spirit – I can't explain it – it's such a wonderful feeling, taking part. It buoys you up, somehow.'

'And that's why you can't keep away from the place?'

'I'm a bit worried about Poison. He's taken a lot of hammer this last week and he looked worn out to start with. Just thought I'd see how he was, and what was happening generally.'

'Before you go to see that punk you can come and explain what you saw to me.'

Tom discovered that Bob's eyes were like needles, and compelling. He wished he'd stayed talking a bit longer to that nice young tourist. But he did as he was told. Together the two men climbed the scaffolding to where Tom and Poison had been sitting together the previous evening.

'The forensic evidence suggests,' said Bob, 'that he was stabbed; and stabbed in the few seconds before he climbed that ladder to the back of the stage. Come on. Re-enact what you did for me.'

Thomas described carefully the scene as he had looked down from the base of the steps leading to his throne in the sky, and a young detective, who had followed them up at a gesture from Bob, took down the names and positions of all the cast as far as Thomas could remember them.

'Then you did what?'

'I stood up, climbed on to the throne, looked down, saw him.'

'Do it for me,' said Bob, producing a stop-watch.

'Quite leisurely, you know,' replied Tom, and demonstrated.

'Leisurely, as you say, but it only took ten seconds until you say he reached the top of the ladder. Let me do it... Yes. I see. Tom, these seconds are crucial. Go through again exactly what you saw. Tell me every detail, no matter how unimportant. Do it again, this time not worrying about how long it took but talking us through it.'

Tom turned his mind back to the previous evening and stated as well as he could who had been on the stage, where they had been standing, what attracted his attention to Exelby ('I happened to look down at my left hand,' he said, without recounting why) and how he had watched him climb the ladder slowly – cross the stage, reeling a little – apparently speak to one of the actors – then fall.

'And Absolom?' snapped Bob.

'Sydney? He wasn't here!'

'But he was. You didn't see him, then? Didn't witness the quarrel?'

'No.' Thomas was shaken. 'It can't be Sydney.'

'Stranger things have happened. The way I have to hear of things! Exelby's secretary talks to the undertaker who talked to the electrician who told him Absolom was here and that there was a flaming row. You know nothing about it. No one else so far has said a thing about it.'

The matter, though, once known, was soon uncovered. The team of detectives and constables had been telephoning and visiting house to house with a questionnaire. 'Did you witness an altercation between Mr Exelby and Mr Absolom?' was hastily added to it, and the audience was included in the people questioned. Locating the different members of the audience added hours of work for the backroom staff.

What the hell had Sergeant Diamond, sitting there among the audience, been doing not to notice it? was the question Bob Southwell was not so much asking as shouting. Sergeant Diamond, much shaken, appeared, to say that he had only joined the audience during the interval. Before that he had been patrolling generally; and it turned out that no member of Task Force had been in the audience before the interval, the danger being expected to be to Poison, and among the cast somewhere.

All the members of Task Force had already made statements about where they were and whom they were with, whom they saw, during the vital time. Busily on duty they had all been, there was no doubt about that. It was unfortunate that the five of them – they were working in shifts and only five of the ten had been on duty just then – did not seem to have been anywhere significant or with anyone acting at all out of character.

One had been in the Tempest Anderson Hall, Sergeant Diamond had been walking the bounds of the Gardens, one had been in the props tent, and the remaining two had been in different parts of St Olave's graveyard with the other members of their groups of Crowd.

The assistant chief constable for Yorkshire arrived, together with Detective Chief Superintendent Duncan.

'We'll be swamped by television crews and intrusive journalists as soon as they know about this,' said Duncan. 'It's bedlam anyway when the festival is on. When the journalists get in on the fact that the director's been murdered, bang go our chances of just quietly finding out who did it.'

'It amazes me that they aren't on to it already.'

The first press conference finally took place

that morning at eleven forty-five, a quarter of an hour after the ACC had arrived, and was the least gruelling of all the many press conferences that were to be held in the course of the next ten days. Word had gone out that the presence of the gentlemen of the press was requested, and a small number of them had come. Although news of the director's death had spread, the full piquancy of the situation had not yet reached the whole of British media.

The announcement was simple and factual. Suspicious death, under investigation by the police. Bare details were given. The bare details were, at that point, enough to make a story and to send the reporters rushing to telephones.

'Well, that's that,' said his chief to Southwell. 'Now wait. Or rather, work like mad to do as much as you can before we're inundated.'

'I've started the interviews and questionnaires already, sir. We've been working since six o'clock.'

'Good man. You've arranged police protection for Peters?'

'He didn't want it, sir.'

'Whether he wants it or not he's got to have it. They're aiming at him, aren't they? We don't want his murder on our heads.'

'We aren't positive they'll try for him next, sir.'

'No, but they might. He's exposed on the stage. If the murderer gets a gun they could pick him off. No problem.'

'We'll do our best, sir.'

'Any idea yet?' the DCS asked Bob Southwell.

'The man originally in charge of stage-lighting, Absolom, has behaved and is behaving oddly. If you remember, Chief, he nearly electrocuted Poison Peters,' ('Good riddance if he had,' grunted the assistant chief constable) 'and he came here to watch the dress rehearsal after being warned off both by Exelby and ourselves; stood up to Exelby's browbeating when he was noticed, and was truculent back; then, did he go quietly and chastened away? He did not. We don't know what he did then, as he's flatly refused to tell us. But he certainly hung around the place.'

'Have you arrested him?'

'I could, if I thought he had anything to do with it. Damn him! He's just muddying the water.'

The water, as far as Bob could see it, was very muddy indeed. It was going to be a long slow job eliminating members of the cast. The audience, apart from Sydney, were in the clear. But even when they narrowed down the suspects, there still remained the possibility that someone from outside – quite unconnected with the plays – had

167

found his way in, hidden under the stage, seized his moment to kill Exelby when for once he was alone, and then got away under cover of the subsequent confusion. Where, in the teeming tourist-swelled city, might he be?

As soon as his talk with Bob Southwell was over, Thomas Churchyard had decided to put off his visit to Poison, and had gone round to see Absolom.

'Well, why shouldn't I have gone to the plays?' Sydney asked aggressively.

'The police told you to keep off the set.'

'I've a right to see the mystery plays same as any other member of the public. And why should I pay for a ticket? All the work I've put in? I just asked the Lady Mayoress if I could join her party. We were at school together and she knows how I've worked for the plays so she said yes.'

'You knew Exelby was bound to see you.'

'And didn't he look small! Bouncing up and down foaming at the mouth with anger just because one innocent old-age pensioner was sitting in the audience.'

'Syd, how could you be so silly? You aren't *any* old-age pensioner. You're the man who nearly electrocuted the star in this production. You and I have known one another in MRS for years but I never knew you'd be so out and out provocative.'

168

'I didn't nearly electrocute him on purpose.'

'You went in the audience on purpose.'

'I've a right to see the mystery plays same as any other citizen of York...'

Tom sighed. Somehow this argument seemed to be going in a circle. He got up from the heavily patterned moquette sofa where Sydney had seated him, and put the half drunk cup of thick tea in its fine china cup ornamented by rampant roses down on a French-polished coffee table.

'I can't do anything with you, Syd. You don't even look as though you're sorry.' And indeed the small cloud of fluffy hair was full of bounce, as if about to take off for an unknown destination. As Tom approached the door on his way out, he saw through the panels of ornamental obscured glass a heavy blue shape with a helmet approaching up the narrow concrete path.

Tom set off back to the Museum Gardens in a mood of black introspection. He paused in a group of people to find out what they were looking at and in front of him a great devil's head sprang into the air, an eruption of evil, filling his vision, startling and shaking him. A medieval play was being enacted on a cart; it was an ordinary enough event at festival time, but he was shaken unreasonably and decided to go and have a beer and a sandwich. Evil, surfacing through brightness, erupting into daylight, had become a reality. Curiously spiky and uncomfortable, it had torn into shreds the bright tapestry of the society in which Thomas lived.

In the warm crowded interior of the Punch Bowl on Stonegate he bought a shepherd's pie and a beer with a whisky chaser, and soon began to feel better. If there was evil in the community it must be rooted out. Then the body politic would be healthy again. He wished he could help. The trouble was he didn't know how to begin. If he knew more clearly what had happened he might be able to think of something...

Bob Southwell had on his desk a number of accounts from people in the audience who had witnessed the director's angry reaction on catching sight of Absolom, the unparliamentary language, the rush down from the stage to pull Absolom up from his seat by the lapels of his raincoat and shake him.

Was that kind of public humiliation – which Exelby seemed only too good at inflicting – enough to make a man commit murder? A quiet, elderly, respectable man? A man disgraced in front of his friends and the leaders of his little community? Was it enough to make him somehow find his way under the stage and strike at the director with a narrow-bladed knife? Combined – Bob reminded

170

himself – with Absolom's resentment of Exelby's importation of Poison Peters?

He was in the middle of interviewing the man. 'So then what did you do?' he asked.

'Went home,' Absolom answered, with much the same nonchalant bravado he had shown to Thomas Churchyard that morning. Bob sighed. He sent two detectives with a search warrant, who combed the tidy little home from insulated loft to neat workshop without finding anything in the least suspicious.

Thomas knocked at the door of Poison Peters's caravan. Poison opened it and stood there looking at him.

'How are you?' asked Tom politely.

Poison made a gesture with his head and turned away leaving the door open; Tom followed him in.

'How are we all, after last night?' Poison asked in reply, putting the kettle on. 'D'yer want tea? I've been drinking gallons.'

'Fine. But I didn't come to beg a cup of tea. I came to ask if you'd like to have a meal with me before the performance tonight. Do you good to get out of this caravan for a bit.'

'Oh, I've been out.' Poison shot Tom a penetrating look from his golden-brown eyes. 'Had a walk round the city centre before breakfast, and finished by the river, watching the birds. The river's all right. Always something different. Not boring. Know what I mean?'

'Not boring – no. Particularly when it floods. I thought a light meal about four o'clock. Soup, salad, fruit, that sort of thing. Unless you go in for steak and chips before a performance.'

'Walk along?' asked Poison.

'Why not? You could walk along the river path. If you're dressed as you are now you shouldn't be recognized.'

With his hair hanging limply, no make-up, washed-out jeans, Poison could have been anybody. Seemingly unable to feel happy without a large symbol on his chest, he was wearing a scarlet T-shirt printed with a huge devil-like head in black surrounded by the words, 'Eric Blood-Axe Rules OK'. Tom shuddered as he looked at it, reminded of the devil's head which had shot up in front of him so unexpectedly. Even this ornament only made Poison blend into the background in York, where the design sold in its thousands to tourists every year.

'I don't want to be back late, though, 'cus I've got to practise my meditation and relaxation before a performance,' said Poison.

'I'll have you back on time.'

'What are you down for now, then? Apart from asking me to come for a meal?'

'I came originally to check on my work – a manhole we're enlarging. It's fine so I was coming to see you when Detective Chief Inspector Southwell saw me and wanted to ask me questions.'

Poison spat neatly into the sink. 'I've had that bastard too. Nine o'clock this morning. "Just routine, Mr Peters," he mimicked. '"So that we can eliminate you from our enquiries." I gave you as my alibi, and I expect you gave me. Perhaps we stabbed Exelby together and are making the alibi up.'

'Did you want to stab him?' asked Tom, interested.

'Sometimes. Insolent bastard. All smarmy nice with me and then there'd be that superior tone, as if I was too dim to understand anything. I understand a lot more than Mr Superior Exelby, I could have told him that.'

'He did manage to put people's backs up.'

'Didn't he yours?'

'Not particularly. His manner was pretty brusque and abrupt but he's – he was – such a damn good director you put up with that.'

Poison shrugged.

'How did you know he was stabbed?'

'I was having a walk round last thing last night and saw them find it.'

'Find what?'

'The dagger.'

'You mean you were snooping?'

'You could call it that. I went under the stage and stood in a dark corner and

173

watched them. They had floods and didn't see me. You can't, you know.'

'Anybody could hide under that stage. But the way we all walk under it to get to the entrances and exits it's surprising no one saw the killer yesterday. Look, Poison, don't go under the stage any more. You don't need to. You can manage all your entrances and exits without it. Come to think of it, don't come to my house along the river bank either. I'll fetch you in the car.'

'They can get me anyway, can't they? Like the juice, and the tree?'

'I expect so. But don't ask for trouble. Those two things – the first I'm sure was a genuine accident. The second was that stupid schoolboy, not thinking of the possible consequences. Criminal ignorance if you like, but not criminal intent. Now – if they're aiming for you, why kill Exelby?'

'Those two – the old sparks nutter and the lad from that posh school – he told them both off, right? So they'd a motive for hitting at him then. Doesn't mean they won't try again for me.'

'If you're looking for someone who's been humiliated by Exelby it could be any of us. Look at the way he treated the Virgin Mary.'

'I felt sorry for that chick.'

'Her boyfriend wasn't too pleased about it either. And Jane Bugg, who's been pushing herself forward all week. He told her to go and stand at the back of the group, out of his sight.'

As Thomas left Poison's caravan he decided to walk home. By now it was mid-afternoon. His bike was locked up at work and he could get it any time. Quite a few of the cast were drifting around the set. The public, shut out of the plays' enclosure, were strolling round the gardens and eating sandwiches in the sun; the police were still scouring every blade of grass in case they had missed something in the night, and a steady stream of them were arriving at the incident-post caravan to report progress before knocking off at the end of their shift.

Sydney Absolom stumbled out of the police caravan.

'Tom!' he grabbed at Tom's jacket. 'They think I've done it. They suspect me. They're going to arrest me at any minute.'

'I'm sure they're not. You're shaking. I'll take you home. Which seems to be becoming a habit.'

Sydney was still shaking.

'I'm perfectly all right.' The older man straightened his spine. 'I've got my shopping to do. I haven't got the joint yet and it's Saturday. I suppose if they arrest me I won't have to bother. They'll have to feed me in prison. That will serve them right. It will save me money as well.'

'Sydney, how long have you and I known

each other?'

'Ten years in June.'

'Is it? Well, it's a long time anyway. I never thought I'd see you behaving like a wet hen.'

Sydney let go of Tom's sleeve, smoothed down his hair with a thin nervous hand, and began to check that he had got everything. Shopping bag, glasses, wallet.

'No need to concern yourself, Mr Churchyard,' he said at last. 'No need at all.'

'Syd!' But like an offended stork Sydney Absolom went alone to the entrance of the partition and was let out by the constable on duty.

Tom went home.

It was a relief to turn into his own quiet avenue. As he walked past the Southwells' new house Linda saw him through the window, and came out to intercept him.

'Tom, can you tell me of a good plumber?'

'What's the matter?'

'Oh, nothing much. Just that there's a stop tap in the bathroom – I'm not sure what it's for – and it keeps dripping. There's quite a wet patch on the carpet and I don't like it. Plumbers aren't busy at this time of year are they? I thought one might look at it.'

'The summer is when they're putting in central heating,' replied Tom. 'Have you pointed it out to Bob?'

'Well I did mention it but he's so busy I don't think he even heard me.'

'Should I have a look?'

'I'd be pleased if you would.'

Tom went up to the bathroom. It was rather small, so Linda had to stand at the door and point the problem out by remote control, as it were. There was a nasty wet patch under the stop tap.

'I know what this stop tap is for – it's for the shower. Mrs Spartan showed me the shower after she'd had it put in and she mentioned it.' He twisted the tap closed. 'There – that stops it dripping, only now you can't use the shower.'

'That's no use,' said Linda. 'It's ideal for this weather. The children are under it every day.'

Thomas was kneeling on the floor peering at the tap. 'I think I have a bit of tow in the garage,' he said. 'That would stop it. It's quite a simple thing. Hardly warrants calling out a plumber. I'll go and fetch it.'

'Thanks,' said Linda.

With a little tow wrapped round inside the tap obligingly stopped dripping.

'That should be all right.' Tom got up, gathered his odds and ends, and prepared to go. 'When you have anything else you want a plumber for, get him to look at it while he's here, but you shouldn't need to send for him specially.'

'It is good of you, Tom. Will you stay for tea?'

'No thanks. I've got a guest for a meal myself – have to go and get something ready towards it.'

During the day reporters of various sorts and kinds descended on York. Camera crews from both BBC and ITV were busy filming the Museum Gardens from every angle. The set was barred to them, as was the Tempest Anderson Hall and the St Olave's parish room. But to be going on with they had plenty of material in St Mary's Lodge and the other buildings, and the place was filled with enthusiastic and personable young men and women speaking earnestly into microphones, the cameras rolling.

The national newspapers had sent up ace reporters, and camera flash bulbs were flashing all over the place.

The police investigating team on house-to-house questionnaire duty were only hours ahead of the newshounds who would presently be going over all the same ground again. The city was already full of tourists; now it became impossible to find a hotel bed inside the old city walls.

Tom drove Poison out to Clifton in his vintage Rolls without either of them talking. There was too much to think about: fear and horror and sudden death and brightness and sunshine and the pavements busy with people of all colours and from many different countries; the roar of traffic and the quiet of Bruce Exelby as he had lain on the stage; the fact that they were alive and hungry and that somewhere there was a killer, who might not have stopped yet.

Tom left the car parked in the road.

'Nice,' Poison patted the mudguards.

'One has to have one extravagance in life.' Tom sounded defensive.

'Why not? Why stop at one?'

On the doorstep was a packet. Tom unwrapped it and found an orange cake with icing, and a message, 'Thank you from Linda.' He smiled. The little neighbourly things which make up everyday life in Ouse Avenue were doubly precious in their contrast to the horror of sudden death.

Poison made himself at home. He walked into the sitting-room, and looked round critically. The walls and curtains were all pale grey though of different textures; the walls smooth and semi-gloss, the curtains velvet. Over the fireplace the chimney breast was papered with a large design of bright tulips on a background of grey, with dark grey leaves. The carpet and furniture were old; a patterned square of carpet with a dark-blue ground, an old-fashioned suite in small-patterned blue velvet. There were lots of bookshelves on either side of the fireplace and a bureau bookcase.

'Got any music?' he asked.

Thomas obligingly fished around and found Britten's 'Noe's Fludde', and put it on. 'That sharp enough for you?' he asked.

Poison looked at him. 'You don't like my type of music, then?'

'I don't much like the sort you make, no. I like the medieval stuff you were playing in the caravan.'

'You're another one who didn't want me to come to York.'

'Not at first. But I didn't know you then. That public image you work so hard at is a bit off-putting. Look, come into the kitchen and tell me what you'd like to eat. We can still hear the music in there.'

'We eating here?' asked Poison, lounging into the kitchen.

'If you like. Or in the dining-room.'

'I like it here. I like that lion you've got on the wall.'

'That's left over from the family who used to live here, like a lot of other things. The place felt homely so I left it alone. The children must have put that poster up.'

Poison walked to the stove and inspected the soup. 'It isn't that powdered stuff, is it?' He sounded doubtful. 'What's it got in?'

'Just fresh vegetables. I like making my own soup.'

'That's all right then. Salad's all right too. What's with it?'

'Salami – cheeses – cold roast beef...'

'Any cottage cheese?'

'Yes.'

'I'll have that, and the salad, and a glass of water, and wholemeal bread if you've got any.'

'Fussy, aren't you?'

'All right! All right! Only checking. I can't eat additives, you see. Allergic, I am. Have to be careful.'

They ate the simple but satisfying meal and Tom drove Poison back to his caravan in plenty of time for his relaxation and meditation, or whatever.

Tom was still concerned about Poison Peters, worried about his safety, wondering how he would find the courage to act in the plays, knowing that a killer was at large and presumably hated him. But when the time came Poison emerged from his hour's relaxation and contemplation in the caravan pale but composed, and dressed in the Tempest Anderson Hall with the rest of them. Tom spoke, but Poison was now withdrawn; he smiled, close-lipped, and that was that. They were all tense.

In less than quarter of an hour the first performance of the mystery plays would begin. There was a kind of light excitement in the air of the city, an electric sparkle generated by the crowds of brightly dressed tourists, and the office girls in their holiday frocks.

The cast were all assembled on the grass in front of the stage. Another minute and the door would be opened to admit the audience. Bob Southwell stood in front of them, for it was the first opportunity he had had to speak to all of them together.

'The position is this: when Bruce Exelby staggered up those stairs to the stage he had just been stabbed by someone. You were all around at the time. I'm not saying that you are all under suspicion of murder. It could have been an outsider, hiding in a dark corner under the stage and awaiting his opportunity. But for your own sakes, I must eliminate as many as possible of you from suspicion as soon as we can. That's why you've been undergoing all this questioning today, and why it's going to go on tomorrow, and probably every day until we find the murderer. You do understand that, don't you?'

They said they did. Everyone wanted to be cleared of suspicion. At present they were looking round at their neighbours, wondering... They didn't know, of course, that they would never be eliminated from suspicion – no matter how good their alibi – until the murderer was found.

'Right,' said Bob. 'The performances are to go on just as if nothing had happened.

182

But for heaven's sake be careful. Be on your guard. The violence might not have ended. Bear with us. We will be as little trouble as we can. Good luck, everyone.' He and the ACC were to sit in the front seats and watch the performance. They were both more nervous than the performers themselves. Would it go through without incident?

The members of the audience came in, carrying their vacuum flasks and their hot-water bottles and their umbrellas and their cushions and their travelling rugs, and settled on the tiered seats. The day was still warm; a perfect June day. Blue sky with small clouds scattered across it as though balls of Sydney Absolom's hair had come adrift and floated into the firmament; a light breeze moving the leaves of the graceful trees in the gardens; flowers in bloom; the stir of the city, the cries of the peacocks, and the lapping of the river in the background.

In spite of rehearsals, tonight was the night. Things could go wrong. The audience out there had paid to see a great theatrical performance and – in spite of everything – that must be what they were to get.

There were many members of the cast who had the greatest possible reluctance to walk under the lower stage, or to approach that strangely clean area on its surface...

Tom walked to centre stage before the play began, and held up his hands for silence.

'Ladies and gentlemen! Before we begin, the cast would like you to join with us in one minute's silence in tribute to our director, Bruce Exelby, so abruptly taken from life yesterday. May we keep silence, please.'

Before the silence fell, there were two full seconds of murmuring surprise. Except for a squawk from a child or two ('They shouldn't bring them so young,' thought Thomas) it was then completely quiet. The far shriek of a fire engine hurrying along High Ousegate came clearly.

After the silence Tom left the stage and went up to his niche in the arches; he had decided not to use the gilded throne in the sky except for the Last Judgement. The audience had arranged its rugs and cushions and hot-water bottles about its many persons and now was quiet again for his opening words.

There was that incredible, magical leap. At one moment Thomas was a telephone engineer, dressed in a funny outfit, standing on scaffolding behind some ruined masonry. In the next second he became transformed. He lifted up his arms, and spread them to embrace the world. An imposing figure, he became God; and began, 'I am Maker Unmade, all might is in me...'

They stopped being actors. They were the Angels, they were Lucifer, they were Devils, they were Adam and Eve in the world's dawn, they were the People of the City portraying the springs of the world and all of life that was therein. The arches, dark against the gradually glowing beauty of an unearthly sunset, the flights of steps, the flat raised areas, the grass in front, were the Heaven and the Earth.

8

Keep thy tunge, thy tunge, thy tunge;
Thy wikked tunge werked me wo.
There is none goes that groweth on ground
Satenas ne peny-round,
Werse than is a wikked tunge
That speketh bothe evil of friend and fo.
Medieval English Verse

It was the day of the second performance.

Jane Bugg had been into the incident room and talked at length.

'I had to tell them about seeing Absolom near the props tent,' she remarked virtuously to Sally Vause, Velvet Smith and an assortment of female Crowd in St Olave's parish room where they were all sitting round having coffee. Although it was Sunday, with a performance to do many of the cast and the supporting team had brought picnic lunches down and were spending the day in town.

'Why did you *have* to tell him?' asked Sally. 'No one supposes for a minute that he would commit murder.' She passed her mug to Velvet for a fill-up.

'*You* might not suppose it – all pals together, aren't you – you members of MRS?

187

Wouldn't do for us all to be so cliquey.' Her broad unpleasant face looked around her.

'We're not in MRS,' remarked an Angel.

'You're too young to be in anything, you're still at school.'

'I expect you think we're cliquey too, Miss Bugg,' said one of the Angels cheekily.

'We're not cliquey,' exclaimed the first, and the half-dozen of them began to chase one another around the hall, dodging in and out of the racks of costumes, shouting to one another,

'I'm not cliquey!'

'Yes you are cliquey!'

'Cliquey!'

'Cliquey!' … until the row was deafening.

'Ignore them,' yelled Sally Vause. 'We're a very friendly society, MRS, though, Jane. Anyone can join. I've often wondered why you don't. We are the Medieval Reconstruction Society and you enjoy this kind of thing so much.'

'Enjoy it? Well – one feels an obligation, you know – to the community – to take part in these things. If one is capable of serving in a particular way one should not be held back by the fear of putting oneself forward.'

'You haven't been,' said Velvet, *sotto voce*.

'*Bruce* was so keen for me to take part. "What shall I do without you, Jane?" he said to me. Poor innocent Bruce. What animal could kill him?'

'He did put people's backs up,' said Sally. 'Of course, he wasn't alone in doing that.'

'Some people have a gift for it,' agreed Velvet, gazing intently at Jane Bugg.

'He was so flattering,' went on Jane as though no one else had spoken. 'So kind of him to place so much reliance on me. I could only do my best to live up to such trust.'

'Trust can be misplaced,' said Velvet, then got up abruptly and took the mugs over to the sink in the corner and washed them viciously, clashing them together.

Sally reflected that for Jane Bugg her public humiliation at Bruce Exelby's hands might never have happened. He had been annoyed by her constantly pushing herself forward, on a number of occasions; but for her to forget how roughly he had told her to keep out of sight at the back of the crowd – well, Sally couldn't have forgotten and forgiven. She wondered if Velvet could. She doubted it, and turned to ask her. But Velvet was washing up again.

The Angels had calmed down. They came and sat again as part of the circle, but the calm did not last long, because a car drew up outside, driven by a parent, and a group of Devils piled out of it and into the parish room.

They had not yet assumed their Devils' dress, and still looked like typical nicely brought-up English fourth formers, in Tshirts, jeans and trainers.

The effect on the Angels, though, was drastic.

'We're not staying here while you're changing,' said the blonde plump Angel, aggressively.

'Wouldn't notice if you were here or not,' retorted one of the boys...

There was a general mêlée. One small Angel shrieked. A Devil was jostling a medium-sized Angel with the apparent intention of twisting her arm behind her back. The dark Angel who enjoyed Chaucer and a more serious Devil were standing together, discussing the different chemistry experiments they had been doing.

'Break it up,' said Sally firmly. 'Go on, you Angels, it's not raining. Go along to the graveyard. It's lovely there under the trees, so peaceful and shady. Velvet, come and help me with these Devils. Did you get the damaged mask back?'

The boys liked wearing their masks. They had been built up on a foundation of old motor bike helmets, so were easy to put on. Once on though, vision was restricted to the great long slit eyes, which because down the plastic of the visors, reflected light and darkness so that at times in the production they were black holes and at other times seemed to dance fire. Although they were only supposed to put on these masks at the end of their spectacular tumbling descent down the long slope from Heaven, they liked them so much they wore them whenever they could, with the aim of frightening as many people as possible.

Velvet produced the damaged mask, which she had retrieved from the props tent that morning. The right horn, carelessly banged against a wall, once more curved up bravely.

The female Crowd including Jane Bugg had left the hall upon the advent of the boys, so, used to the presence of Sally and Velvet, they changed noisily into their devilish outfits. Once in, they were completely covered in red and black; but then they put on their white angelic robes. These had been specially made so that they could be shed instantly at the moment of their being cast out from Heaven; the boys emerged from them leaving the robes scattered like split banana skins on the downward slope.

'I say, Miss Smith,' said one. 'Is it true then that old Exelby was murdered?'

'The police are investigating his death,' said Velvet.

'That means he was murdered, doesn't it? We might get murdered as well!'

'I wouldn't be surprised.'

'Who'd want to murder him? Now if it had been old Pikey' – naming their form master as none but they knew him – 'that would be all right–'

'I'd murder Pikey,' said one boy with relish. 'I'd boil him in oil and give him the death of the thousand cuts and blow him up with a car bomb and vaporise him with a laser gun.'

'Take no notice of him,' said a larger Devil patronizingly to Velvet. 'He's only Lower Fourth. Very lower, and very fourth-rate, Jones Minor, aren't you? Sound more like a first former. Be your age.'

'Be your age yourself! I saw you talking to Louise.'

The racket was still going on as the group of six Devils pushed out of the door of the parish room. Encumbered by their angel drapings and their padded tails which tended to stick out of the white robes at the back they solved the problem of what to do with their masks by putting them on their heads. Wearing their costumes made them into anonymous creatures and freed their inhibitions, if they had ever had any.

The disgrace of one of their number for his stupid and dangerous escapade with the branch and the bolt from the cross had not quelled them. Even the stately eldest of them revelled in being a child again, skipping, jumping, banging a smaller boy up against the walls of the lane which ran towards Marygate. With a sort of chorus of wild yells they plunged and swooped in a crazy progress.

'Thank goodness they've gone,' said a left-over female Crowd, who had been un-noticed in a corner, getting up and shaking out her long medieval kirtle. 'I should think you're tired out in here when you've got rid of everyone.'

'You've said it,' said Sally.

'That Jane Bugg! Isn't she poisonous?'

'Positively so,' agreed Velvet. 'Some one ought to stick a knife in *her*.'

'Is that what they did to Mr Exelby? At least the weather's fine so far. These woollen things smell sheepy when they're wet. I really feel as if I'm back in the Middle Ages then. Remember the last time the plays were per-formed, when we kept on getting drenched? And Bruce Exelby hasn't done us any favours, saying we haven't to wear under-clothes. Not that I took any notice.'

'What he said was he didn't want any nylon frills peeping out or long thermal underpants.'

'Well, fair enough. But if he thought I'm having wool next to my bare skin he'd an-other think coming. My skin's very sensitive. I've got bra and panties and vest and tights on.'

'You shouldn't really have a bra,' remon-strated Sally. 'It doesn't give the correct medieval droopy look.'

'You look fine,' Velvet cut in sharply.

This was the lady in the Crowd who carried a spindle and had already during rehearsals spun enough yarn for a woolly hat. She was hoping by the end of the plays to have enough for a matching scarf at least. Although she chatted brightly she always seemed half abstracted as she drew on her thread and watched the descending spindle. Yet it was she who produced the new bit of evidence.

'I saw Mr Absolom that night,' she said now, giving the spindle a twist to set it moving. 'I think it's awful the way Jane Bugg just called him 'Absolom' without the Mr.'

'How do you mean, you saw him?'

'After that row with Bruce Exelby. I saw him hanging around the props tent.'

'You'd better tell the police,' advised Sally.

'Oh, don't worry. I'm going to. As soon as they get round to interviewing me.' She twirled again. The spindle spun round. Everyone's eyes were on her, standing there with that assiduously withdrawn look. Just what, and how much, had she seen?

'Of course, as I said to the police,' Jane Bugg remarked, 'the Virgin Mary was very upset. Are you better now, dear? It must have been dreadful for you, poor Bruce going off at you like that. I did explain it all to that nice detective. "He'd thought she showed such promise," I said, "and had such hopes for her. It was very natural for her to get upset, even if she did go to extremes. Young people

194

are very melodramatic, especially if they imagine they've got theatrical talent. I've seen it so often. As we get older we learn a few lessons. But when we're that age it all means so much to us, we are likely to go off the deep end and do over-dramatic things." That's what I said to them, my dear. I did stick up for you as much as I could.'

The Virgin Mary's mouth had gradually been falling open as she listened.

'What do you mean?' she gasped out at last. 'What were you talking to the police about me for, you old bag?'

'You mustn't be abusive, dear. That won't be for your own good at all. They only asked me if I had seen anyone behaving in a peculiar manner. And you must admit, dear, your behaviour was very peculiar when dear Bruce just said a little word to you.'

It was fortunate that at that moment Mary could not speak at all.

'I did what I could to excuse you, my dear,' ended Jane, smiling beatifically, giving the Virgin Mary's arm a little pat before walking away through the gravestones.

'Pity no one murdered *her*,' murmured a female Crowd, looking anxiously at the Virgin Mary. Suddenly Mary burst out into wild irrepressible laughter. A group gathered round her. The laughter changed to tears, paused, broke, continued.

'She's hysterical,' someone said. 'Some-

195

body do something. Where's a first-aider?'

'She's told them I did it,' sobbed Mary, then laughed in a kind of shriek. 'She must be mad. Stop her somebody. I didn't do it.' She wept. A motherly woman in a russet woollen gown gathered the girl into her arms and for a few seconds she sobbed heart-brokenly on the edges of the cream wimple. Then she broke away and let out a scream. 'She's accused me!' she cried.

'Look, this isn't helping,' said someone.

Thomas Churchyard joined the group – they opened to let him in, looking at him anxiously, sure he could help, relying on his dependable aura. Tom felt far from capable of coping with the situation. He knew hysterical people ought to be slapped. So did everyone else in the group. No one had had the courage to do it.

'Fetch a glass of water,' Tom said sharply to a lad in jerkin and hose who was at his elbow. 'Run to the police caravan, they'll have one.' He turned to Mary. 'This won't do,' he said, but she was wailing wildly.

Tom slapped her twice, lightly but sharply. The noise stopped as if someone had flipped a switch. Her blue eyes looked at him, dazed and blank.

'You're hysterical. No need for that.'

The boy arrived with the water.

'Drink this,' said Thomas, 'and be quiet for a minute.'

The motherly woman took Mary's wrist and felt her pulse.

'You'd better have a hot drink, something warm round you, and be alone for half an hour,' she said.

'There isn't time...' the nervous tone rose in Mary's voice.

'There's plenty of time. We can find a side room in the Tempest Anderson.' Mary let herself be led off.

The group who had gathered round her dissolved, either to regroup with others, or to drift away.

Thomas went in search of Jane Bugg.

He did not get the chance to reproach her with upsetting Mary, for she waded into him at once.

'I wanted to have a word with you, dear Thomas. Thank heavens you've come. The police suspect me – I know they do, some of the things they said. Just because dear *Bruce* scolded me a little. As if I minded that! If he needed to let off steam far better on me – his old friend and colleague – than on some of these over-sensitive melodramatic creatures. Still, as I said, they led me to think they suspect me – but I saw Absolom behaving in a very peculiar manner.'

'What was Mr Absolom doing?' Tom couldn't help himself. Defending Mary would have to wait.

'I had to tell the police of course. How

could I keep it to myself? I saw him acting in a very peculiar manner, I said to them. But then he's a very peculiar man. His appearance, to start with. That mack he always wears. And that funny hair. And that nervous way his hands twitch about.'

Thomas thought Jane Bugg's appearance left much to be desired, but he didn't say so. 'I like Mr Absolom's appearance,' he said, 'but of course people's appearance in general one likes or dislikes as a matter of taste. The police are hardly likely to be influenced by your not liking the way Mr Absolom looks.'

'But I saw him acting in a most peculiar manner. It was after the row. He was supposed to leave the place. "*Go!*" dear *Bruce* told him.' She showed how, with theatrically outstretched finger and deepened voice. '*Go!* and don't come near the plays again." But did he go? No, he did not. He lurked. He lurked around the props tent. And where else could he have got that dagger? That was where that wretched Devil found the willow branch. The props tent is full of all sorts of lethal objects.'

'Your tongue will get you into trouble, Jane,' said Thomas. '"Alle bakbiteres hi wendeth to helle."'

He felt infinitely weary. Telling her off seemed like too much effort. He turned and left her, and went over to the props tent.

The props tent had a look of impermanence, a gaiety, missing from the rest of the scene. The willow branches for the day were leaning against one side, the tall spears with their hardboard blades glittering with silver paint leaned against the other.

'Build me a willow cabin at your gate,' thought Thomas. A curtain of large felt leaves strung on strong thread and suspended from a rope between two coat stands obscured the door.

Inside it was dim but light, as it is in tents. There was a table strewn with the materials of the prop-maker's trade – Stanley knives, pots of glues, paintbrushes, aerosol sprays of various substances, scissors and a pincushion full of pins. A crown was in the centre having its topmost jewel re-attached, and one of the Three Kings was standing by looking anxious and filling what empty space there was with his robes of brown and gold.

Behind the tables a calm-looking woman was carefully wiping away surplus glue. She looked up quickly as Thomas entered. She was a small neat person, all rounded shapes in a shirt and jeans and flat sandals.

'I'll wait,' said Thomas. At that she dismissed him from her thoughts and concentrated again completely on the job in hand. It seemed to take a long time. At last the King departed joyfully and she turned her attention to Thomas. He came to the conclusion that she was a painter. No other people rivet one with that impersonal stare.

'Yes?' she asked.

'Er ... on the night of the murder...' he started, hesitant.

'I was in here. Always am in here. Live in this place. Told the police and the journalists so. Nothing else to say.'

'I hear Sydney Absolom was seen hanging about here after Mr Exelby threw him out of the audience.'

'He may have been. I didn't see him.'

'No chance of him – er – pinching a Stanley knife or–'

'I did go out for a coffee and a break,' admitted the woman, 'during the interval. Told them that. Nothing missing. The dagger wasn't ours. Wouldn't have cut anyone if it had been ours, because if a dagger had been needed we'd have made it of hardboard,' she added with the first touch of humour.

'Oh. Right. Thanks.'

'Anyway it's not me that leaves my post. You want to have a talk to those wardrobe people. Whenever you want them they're never in St Olave's parish room.'

'They have to look after the costumes in the Tempest Anderson as well, you see,' he said defending his members of MRS, Sally Vause and Velvet Smith.

He withdrew. She had already forgotten him. As the felt leaves of the Garden of Eden brushed past his face, he glanced back and saw that she was completely absorbed again, drawing a shape on a piece of paper. He felt that the props tent was as much a bit of another world, dropped down from the sky or somewhere, as was Poison's caravan or the police incident post. Except that the props tent came direct from an older world than anything else – a world before the medieval, when the Little People sang under the Hollow Hills.

It seemed perfectly in keeping that this was the place where silly innocent Sydney Absolom had been seen 'lurking about'.

Somewhere else evil was lurking, hidden under some fair exterior; it was like an abscess, out of sight, poisoning the whole. Would he sense it? He could sense it – running near him; spoiling for him like an underground cesspit the pure pleasure of being involved in the mystery plays.

Sydney Absolom was walking through the Museum Gardens, minding his own business, looking longingly at the tall fence round the play area, when he met Jane Bugg.

'Oh, Sydney!' she said. 'What do you think to all this? It's all very peculiar. You must be glad you were out of the way before it happened.'

He gave her a glum look. 'I was still here. The police suspect me,' he said.

'Nonsense, Sydney. They know you didn't have anything to do with it. Even if you are a member of MRS. They're bound to suspect you all, of course.'

'What do you mean?'

'You're all in it, aren't you? All involved in the plays? And some of you knew dear poor *Bruce* when he was in York many years ago. Don't try to fob *me* off, Sydney. You know jolly well who I mean. Wasn't there someone *rather* close to him? Oh, I was new in York then and of course you were all born here. But I remember the gossip very well. She did nothing but talk about him in those days. It was "Bruce is going to do this and Bruce is going to do that". I can see why you tried to electrocute him, Sydney, wicked though it was of you. I told the police I could see why you'd done it. You were expressing your sympathy for her, weren't you? I didn't tell them that of course. Just that I could see why you'd done it. They didn't ask anything else on that point. But you and I know, don't we, Sydney?'

'You think I really tried to electrocute him, Jane? You haven't been and told them that?'

'I said it was very understandable, Sydney dear. Old loyalties die hard, don't they, dear?'

'Don't you think it's bad enough being suspected, Jane Bugg, without having you push your oar in? And goodness knows what you're talking about or think you've remembered.'

'Well of course I'm not good enough for you. Not a member of your famous MRS, am I? You're too exclusive for that. Well, this is what I think of you all, you superior lot!' And Jane spat on the ground.

'Jane!' Absolom, who was unmarried and had a high ideal of women, looked revolted. 'Jane! You forget yourself. You would have been welcome to join MRS at any time. Tom could have told you that.'

'Do you think I would have wanted to join you, you murdering crew?' cried Jane. '*Bruce* was worth all eleven of you. Bruce knew how to value the help of a lady. Bruce relied on my help. I wish you would explain that to the police, Sydney dear. They seem to think I had a grudge against him. So silly.'

9

We get no rest until this thing
Be brought to end.

The Skynners' Play

The assistant chief constable was giving a press conference. He hated doing it. His uniform was hot and uncomfortable and middle age was thickening his neck, so that the size sixteen collars were now a little too tight. He could think of things he would rather be doing on a warm June day than facing a ravening horde of journalists and photographers. It wasn't as though he could tell them of any startling progress, or indeed of anything much at all...

'Yes, we have found the murder weapon. Yes, you may use the photographs of it which we will be issuing to you. No, there were no fingerprints on it, it has yielded no evidence at all.

'Are we looking for someone showing scratches and with bloodstained clothing? No, we are not. There was no skin under Exelby's fingernails and no sign that he resisted his attacker. We think he was taken by surprise.

'This may indicate that he knew his attacker, yes. It may only indicate that he was just standing there, or walking, and the attack was so swift and unexpected that he did not have time to react. Someone passing stabbed him, withdrew the stiletto, threw it away, left him. It must have been as simple as that.

'Why aren't we expecting bloodstains on the attacker? Well, puncture wounds of this type don't bleed much. In fact it was not until he had collapsed on stage that he really bled.

'As to why Exelby was murdered... No, we don't know. Yes, our first thought was that it must be in connection with his choice of Poison Peters to take the part of Christ.

'We still consider that the strongest possibility.

'Other possibilities we are considering? Exelby was a very dominating personality and caused a certain antagonism wherever he went.

'Whether the antagonisms were a sufficient motive for murder is what we have to find out.

'No, I certainly don't mean that the cast of the mystery plays is riven by dissension, and all at each other's throats. I understand theatrical productions always create a great deal of tension between the various members of the cast. In my judgement the mystery plays have less of this than ordinary performances, because of the whole nature and theme of the plays. As theatre goes they are a remarkably united and harmonious cast.

'A suspect? Until the murderer is found we must suspect everyone who could have been in the right place at the right time.

'You are quite right in your supposition that the director lived for a while after the wound was inflicted. He lived for about two and a half minutes.'

A reporter asked if Exelby had said anything.

'Said anything?' Here the assistant chief constable for Yorkshire paused. He turned to Bob Southwell, who was sitting at his side. 'Did he say anything, Bob?' he asked quietly.

Bob replied just as quietly. 'Yes, he was speaking.'

One of the more intrusive and cheeky of the journalistic bunch shouted out, 'What's that? Speak up! Let us all hear!'

At the request of his superior Bob rose and took the microphone.

'Yes is the answer to your question. As Bruce Exelby crossed the stage he passed close to the actor playing Isaiah, and seemed to be trying to speak to him. The only word the actor could catch appeared to be "father?". He said that Exelby's tone was questioning. That is all he was heard to say.

What the significance of it is I only wish *you* could tell *me.*'

At this slight touch of levity the gentlemen of the press shouted with laughter and Bob's popularity soared. He gave the microphone back to the assistant chief constable and sat down again.

Bob's levity had gone when he and the ACC were alone together after the press conference, sharing a percolator-full of rather bitter coffee in the partitioned-off end of the police mobile incident post.

'The opposition to Poison included good and responsible sections of the community,' remarked the ACC. 'Could any of these apparently decent people tip over into fanaticism and actually commit murder?'

'It sounds possible, put like that,' Bob answered. 'It's baffling because there's so little to go on,' he went on. 'No fingerprints, no scratch marks on the assailant, no fibres, and so many people were around the place. It can't have been easy to find him alone and in a secluded spot, actually. The AD was with him most of the time, walking behind taking instructions.'

'AD?'

'Assistant director. Sue Brown. Though she was sent off pretty often to fetch sandwiches and all kinds of other rather trivial jobs. But whoever did it was lucky to find him alone and in a place where they were not observed... Exelby spent a lot of time in front watching the action, or charging up on stage saying, "Do it like this". It was his last night but one in York. If they had not struck when they did it might have been much more difficult on the actual first night.'

'Motive,' put in the ACC.

'Motive? – how big a motive does anyone need for murder? Religious fanaticism? The word tells us that can be a motive, though the good burghers of York seem unlikely to be so carried away... Is it enough to be slighted and shown up before your fellows in a thing which is, after all, make-believe? No, don't get me wrong. I'm a Christian. But any play must be make-believe, whether or not the events it portrays are true. Is it enough to have someone you disapprove of cast as the living God? Is it enough to have someone make a pass at your girlfriend? Are these big enough motives for taking a life?'

'They might be if the person's mind is unhinged.'

'Unhinged. Or in the heat of temper. Or in cold deliberation of planned purpose.'

There was a pause between the two men. That last had not been spoken before.

'It's a needle in a haystack,' said the assistant chief constable in his weighty voice.

'The only thing is to keep on looking. To sift the haystack until we find the needle.'

'If it's someone unhinged they might do

209

some other mad, useless thing. Have you got that protection on Poison Peters? If it was because of him, he's in danger. Even though nothing was tried last night that could be to put us off our guard.'

'I've got him to have a personal bodyguard. Though it wasn't easy. He isn't persuadable and doesn't like me. He doesn't want his privacy threatened. For my part, I'd just like to know what *does* go on in that caravan of a night.'

'And if it was your second reason, in the heat of temper. Then there must have been something to trigger off the explosion. The person must have seemed agitated either before or after, and surely that would have been noticed. Either agitated or unusually silent and white.'

'It could have been a number of people then. Exelby upset the Virgin Mary, and therefore by implication her boyfriend, the Youngest Shepherd; the Porteress, and others. So far the only person fitting your pattern of agitation is Sydney Absolom.'

'He who muddies the water? Don't reject him out of hand, Bob. The obvious is often the solution.'

'Right.'

'Now we come to your third hypothesis. The cold deliberation of planned purpose. Doesn't that seem the most likely? With no clues left behind? No fingerprints? No carelessness? Above all – the *preparedness?* I think someone was watching for their chance, ready for it, prepared for it.'

'Everyone is careless sooner or later,' muttered Bob Southwell.

'Granted. And that's what we as policemen look out for. The tiny telltale carelessness.'

The ACC often lectured to recruits. The phrases he used to them tended to slip out at less appropriate moments. 'But let's think further about this. Cold deliberation. Planned purpose. This might have its roots far back in time, long before this performance of the mystery plays, long before Exelby's choice of Poison Peters. Detach someone from the team and set them to finding out about his past life, Bob.'

'I already have done that, sir.'

'He was a man who made enemies, who bear him grudges. The chap you have detached might come up with a lot of possibilities.'

'Not so many when you think of the person with a grudge has also got to be here in York now.'

'Could be a contract killing.'

'Contract? He isn't a gangland boss.'

'No. But you don't know what you might uncover. Stage people. Was he involved with drugs for instance?'

'There's one thing,' Bob brightened. 'Fingerprints, none. Either the murderer took time to wipe the weapon clean very carefully, so that not even the tiniest fragment of a print was left anywhere. Or else their hands were covered.'

And the only people with regularly covered hands on the set of the mystery plays were the Devils, the arms of whose costumes ended in grotesque gloves, claw-ended, which they used to maximum effect – spreading their fingers and raking the air, making threatening gestures to the lost souls in their care, pointing and dramatically gesturing. And there was the stupid young Devil who had messed about with the cross. Had he sneaked back into the performance? Once in his costume Bruce Exelby would not have recognized him or realized that he had disobeyed orders. It was unlikely anyone would notice a Devil too many. Yet anyone could have put on gloves.

'The main motives for murder, you know,' remarked the assistant chief constable, 'are sex and greed.'

'I had noticed, sir,' replied Bob, thinking to himself that he didn't see how either fitted in this particular case. Exelby had apparently been trying to make the Virgin Mary, before he gave her a public humiliation; he had several times had a flashily pretty girl in tow for the after-rehearsal drink, but never the same one twice; he had been married briefly for six months, and happily divorced ever since. It all gave the impression that what really made him tick was the theatre.

Greed? Blackmail – inheritance after his death – at first sight both seemed unlikely. There was no doubt Exelby had done well, but he obviously spent heavily; West-end flat, glamorous secretary, beautiful luggage, expensive hand-made shoes and exclusive watch. Bob Southwell doubted if there was much left of his earnings when all that lot was paid for. He remembered the Porsche, and thought some men might kill to own one of those – maybe.

He shook his head. Those deliberations hadn't seemed to get him anywhere.

'There's nothing for it, sir,' he said to the assistant chief constable, as though all this had been spoken instead of revolving internally, 'but to go on working steadily away in the normal police manner. Interview all these hundreds of people, tabulate them, computerize the information – see where it gets us.'

'All this technology! Nothing wrong with a pad and pencil.'

'Nothing, sir. But these new tools exist. May as well use them. Apart from anything else, the media criticise us if we don't. They think we're efficient if we use a computer – inefficient if we don't. The fact that the

Yorkshire Ripper was caught by two constables who noticed a wrong number plate and checked up on it, and not by all the computers in the world, doesn't seem to register with them.'

The ACC nodded. 'You go on doing what you're doing, Bob, and I'll try to keep these man-eating media tigers out of your hair. The trouble with computers – I've really nothing against them, mind, we have to move with the times – is that they're still in their infancy and, more to the point, so are we in dealing with them. When all the Force have been using computers since junior school we'll find them a darn sight more useful than we do now, when most of us are only learning the language and what they're capable of. There's never going to be any substitute though for common sense and intelligent observation of trifles. Now – this murder – I'm very much afraid there'll be another attempt, this time on Poison Peters. He's the target, I'm sure of it. *Protect him, Bob.* When did you fix the inquest for?'

'It's to be a week tomorrow, sir. If we're going to get anywhere with this case we should have an inkling by then.'

'I hope so, because that's the outside limit of time I can let you have all this extra manpower.'

It was on the day of that first press conference and of the discussion in the police caravan, in the midst of all the growing furore, that Linda had a real emergency on Ouse Avenue. Tom was in the garden pottering about, and had been chatting to the children, Susan and Paul, over the low post-and-wire fence. They had chased around on their bicycles until they were exhausted and were now flopped on the grass reading, with a pile of books between them.

'What are you reading?' Tom asked.

'We're going to join the police force when we grow up,' explained Susan, 'so we've got Daddy's books out of the bookcase and we're starting to learn about it. We want to find murderers like Daddy does.'

'Doesn't he mind you getting his books?' asked Tom doubtfully. But he didn't like to interfere and Linda – who was papering Paul's bedroom upstairs with a design of sailing ships on a wavy sea – was nowhere to be seen. So Tom got his shears and went to trim his front hedge, wishing the family who had owned his house before him had not planted privet.

He worked for some time and at last gathered all the trimmings together into the wheelbarrow and went round into the back again. As the privet trimmings were still young and softish he decided they would do perfectly well in the compost heap, and was putting them into it when he heard a kind of gasping sound from the next-door garden. It was Susan, who with her hand to her mouth was looking down at something. In a second she turned and ran into the house, crying, 'Mummy! Mummy!'

Thomas moved over quickly to the divide between the gardens, looked over, and saw Paul lying motionless on the grass. He was no quicker than Linda, who flew out into the garden and over to Paul.

She knelt by him, moved her hand over his forehead and took his wrist.

'What's the trouble?' asked Tom, realizing he might be able to help.

'He's unconscious. They've been playing some game...' Linda's voice could hardly stagger out of her lips.

'Ambulance,' said Tom.

'Yes.'

'I'll phone for it.'

An ambulance was fortunately nearby, returning from taking someone home, and was with them in half a minute. Paul, now moaning a little, was lifted into it, and Linda went with him. Everything happened so quickly it was incredible. Tom stood there holding Susan's hand. 'I'll look after her,' he said.

'Don't tell Bob yet,' said Linda. 'I always try not to bother him at work. Paul doesn't seem as deeply unconscious as he did.'

With that the ambulance was on its way.

Tom looked down at Susan. 'What happened, Sue?' he asked.

'I was learning self-defence,' she answered in a small voice. 'Paul told me to practise pressure points on him so I was. Well, I was trying to. I had my arm round his neck, sort of. Then he went all funny.'

'I thought you shouldn't have been looking at grown-up books.'

Susan began to cry in great torrents, and he put his arm round her. 'There's no point in crying,' he said awkwardly. 'Look, let's go inside and wait in the room with the phone. Mummy will soon be ringing to tell us that everything's all right.'

'I've killed him,' sobbed Susan.

'For heaven's sake don't blame yourself, Susan. All sorts of things happen when you're playing. You didn't mean to hurt him, did you? I'm sure he'll be all right.'

He couldn't bring himself to be severe with her while she was in such misery, though he wished he had drawn Linda's attention earlier to the fact that the children had Bob's books in the garden. Remembering the Virgin Mary's hysterics Tom wondered what he had done to deserve the sole care of weeping females.

'Let's go and fetch your Daddy's books inside,' he said at last. 'We can put things right that much, anyway.'

It seemed a long wait for news. The worst

217

of it was that Bob phoned.

'What are you doing there, Tom?' he asked, surprised. 'Changed your job to switchboard operator?'

'Just holding the fort. Linda's had to take Paul to hospital. Nothing to worry about. Susan and I are tidying books away to pass the time.'

It was not so easy to fob Bob off. His voice hardened to that of a practised interrogator. Tom found himself explaining the whole thing, making as light of it as he could. 'Paul was already beginning to recover consciousness,' he explained. 'But you have to take all possible precautions where a child is concerned. He'll be right as rain.'

Bob was in the middle of dealing with the murder enquiry and with the well known personality who was the representative of the regional TV programme *Almanac*. He had to put down the phone and be on view and in action, however sharp his private worry.

'What significance does the Saddlers' Play have, Mr Southwell?' asked the well groomed and glamorous Hermione. 'Why was it in that particularly play that Bruce Exelby was stabbed?'

Bob, thinking of his son lying unconscious and what his wife's agony must have been as she stood beside him, found it was all he could do to answer. But his words came out efficiently and clearly all the same. 'As far as we know it has no significance…'

'This is an angle the police enquiries have taken into account?'

'We try to take all angles into account, Miss Hermione.'

She did not look convinced but took her leave. At once Detective Inspector Smart came in, with sheets of computer printouts to discuss with Bob. Bob thought afterwards that it had been one of the worst half-hours of his life. Ringing in his head were thoughts of the strong manly son he was so proud of and the dainty daughter he cherished. Suppose Paul didn't come round … suppose… DI Smart thought his new boss very keen and super-efficient, and began to fear as well as to respect him.

As well as featuring an item on *Almanac* about the Saddlers' Play, Hermione told a journalist friend of her theory about the significance of the play during which the murder was committed. The friend had gone into this in depth, producing a very long and academic article on the hidden meanings of each play and why, in the opinion of a psychologist, the murderer had chosen the one he did.

Thomas found his time of looking after Susan exhausting. He had managed to stop the worst of her crying by making her help him pick the books up from the grass and return them tidily to the glass-fronted cupboard, though he knew they must be all in the wrong order. But every few minutes she was overcome with remorse and began crying again, wanting to know if Paul would die and if it would be all her fault.

When the phone rang again he snatched it up.

'It's all right,' it was Linda's voice. 'He recovered perfectly and we're coming home. He's had four X-rays of his head and neck and they can find nothing wrong. They think it was pressure on the carotid something or other. I feel as if we'd been here hours. They think to be on the safe side he'd better wear a surgical collar for a few days, but there don't seem to be any after-effects.'

'Do talk to Susan and calm her down a bit,' Thomas begged. 'And Bob rang.'

'You didn't tell him?'

'I didn't have much choice. I had no right to keep it from him.'

'I'll ring him as well. Put Susan on. And thank you, Thomas, you've been a brick.'

'It'll cost you,' said Tom. 'Another orange cake will do nicely.'

Over the next few days, the results of the hundreds of interviews poured into the murder room, where two young police personnel, a man and a woman, sat keying them into the computer. At least, as Bob Southwell said, it seemed to eliminate some people from their enquiries. There were quite a lot of convincing alibis, people who corroborated one another, and whom there was no reason to doubt.

Bob had made light of his worry over Paul's accident, and the boy seemed none the worse. He went around rather proud of the thick white collar protecting his neck. It was really unnecessary, but seeing this precaution made everyone feel better except Susan, who could hardly look at Paul without wanting to cry. She decided to be a nurse instead of a policewoman. It was really Bob who came off worst in the end, for, just when his mind should have been entirely free to concentrate on his work, it kept reverting to his son, and to the ease with which he might have lost him for ever.

Bob had the extra manpower for just four days, before an emergency in another area caused them to be drawn off and left him with his usual team.

'You know most murders are detected in the first forty-eight hours or not at all,' said the ACC.

'Well, you've certainly given us all the help you can, sir. We've got masses of information to sort.'

'I have the feeling this one is going to remain unsolved, Bob. Just nothing to go on.'

But Bob was not willing to believe that.

A plan had been made of the abbey ruins, and one by one dots were placed where people were confirmed as being at the beginning of the Saddlers' Play. There were three overlays; one for the main stage, one for the upper stage, and one for the heights above.

So far only three people were marked on the upper levels. Poison Peters, who had been resting with his head sunk in his arms, recuperating from the crucifixion and preparing for his next entrance; Humphrey Hale the Archangel Gabriel, who had been trying to read a book in the peculiar lighting – half dusk and half stage-floods – with the aid of nips from his hip flask; and Thomas Churchyard, playing God, who had risen, surveyed the scene of shadowed grass, trees and tombstones, climbed to his throne in the sky and looked down at the brightly-lit stage below him.

On the second overlay there was nothing; the upper stage where the cross was had been empty at this period in the plays.

On the third overlay, there were six actors on the lower stage.

The ground plan showed a further eight just off-stage in Hell's Mouth, visible to the actors already on set. Also a number – an uncomfortably large number – in among the graves at the back of the set, in the props tent, or in progress from one place to another. They were all wanted for the finale; and, cool though the evenings became as night deepened, they preferred to be there, listening to the sounds from the plays, than to being anywhere else. In front there was the audience.

On the understage area there was so far only one person, Exelby himself.

Bob stood for a long time seriously studying the dots. He looked at the list at the side of persons whose whereabouts were not yet fixed. Only one name now remained on it – Sydney Absolom. Bob Southwell sighed.

'Of course,' Tom said to him later, 'People did drift round to the front and join the audience from time to time.'

'What sort of people?'

'Oh – props – costumes – make-up – backstage people.'

'And drifted away again, do you mean?'

'Yes.'

'I'm only interested in where they were for that few seconds. You mean someone might have been in the act of drifting back to their post, and taken in Bruce Exelby on the way?'

'I hadn't thought it through.'

'It's possible. It's worth getting the audience to remember if they can, anyone who joined them for a short time, whenever it was. And having a close look at the backstage people. I wonder if any of them escaped questioning? We would tend to assume that they stayed put at their posts, well away from the stage area.'

The press had had a field day after the press conference. Photographs appeared in the national dailies – glamorous photographs of Bruce Exelby, many of them from ten years earlier; photographs of the set and the cast, fortunately in good supply from the photo-call session. Poison came in for a lot of publicity and his agent rushed northwards, to act as a buffer between him and the ravening reporters. Poison refused to face the media. He said he felt that his role demanded all his energy, and outside performances he was husbanding his resources.

'Have you seen the article in the *Guardian?*' Bob Southwell asked his second-in-command. 'No? Well, it's worth looking at. *The Times* virtually ignores us, the tabloids shriek the most melodramatic and inaccurate version they can, but the *Guardian* bloke has been doing a bit of research. Did you know that Exelby had been in York before?'

'Didn't know anything about him.'

'He was here for two years at the beginning of his career.'

'Is it important?'

'It might be. Everything's important. Who

did we put on to tracing his past? James Jester? Give him this article, will you?'

'The electrician chappie is the murderer, surely.'

'Sydney Absolom is a retired grocer with an interest in everything electrical and in local history. He's a mild, conventional man, rooted in his community.'

'So was Crippen,' retorted the other. 'Perhaps apart from the rooted in the community bit, sir. Well – the same kind of man, anyway.'

'He doesn't seem the one, to me.'

'Then there's the Youngest Shepherd – jealous as hell over the Virgin Mary – no one's quite sure whether he was with them just at the right time or whether he was in transit to another group, or snogging with Mary which is where we've put him, it seems the likeliest…'

'I would have agreed with you – that young man is both callow and cocky and I wish I could think that the world would teach him a lesson pretty soon, but somehow I don't think it is going to – until recently the Youngest Shepherd and the Virgin Mary were on the "whereabouts unconfirmed" list, but there were seven well attested sightings of them in a remote corner of the graveyard. Whatever they were doing, they were not taking life.'

'Hmm. Then there's that Devil who

mucked around with the cross. His parents say he was at home, upstairs doing his homework with the radio full on. There's the roof of an extension outside his bedroom and he could have got out of there and later climbed back again without their knowing.'

'I'm considering him, don't worry. All I'm saying is that sometimes murder comes from way back – from something everyone but the murderer has forgotten. Just give that article to James Jester. And find out from that wretched woman playing the Porteress how it was she knew Exelby so well – to hear her talk you'd think they were blood relations.'

''S all right now, yeah,' said Poison.

He was sitting with Thomas and with Humphrey Hale, theYoungest Shepherd, and the Virgin Mary, round a table in a dark corner in one of the pubs in Marygate. They were a week into the production, with two weeks still to go. 'I've got over the beginning a bit.'

Thomas thought, without saying so, that Poison was more relaxed today than he had ever seen him.

'You had a rough time,' said Humphrey Hale sympathetically.

'Yeah – being called a blasphemer and all that. Folks saying "He thinks he's good enough to play Christ."'

'They don't think what they're saying,'

soothed Thomas.

'Too right they don't think about it,' said Poison, fishing the slice of lemon out of his Malvern water. 'If they'd felt like I did going for that audition they'd know. I was shit-scared when I was asked. Then as I went along I felt all this aggro – you know – what the hell are they after? Why me? Are they taking the mick? I nearly turned round and went back.'

'I felt a bit like that,' chipped in the Virgin Mary. 'I'd only gone with Louise – you know she's my young cousin, don't you – and the rest of her gang hoping I'd be an Angel, and they were only going because Louise's sweet on one of the Devils. Then they picked me out to read for Mary. I wanted to find a hole to crawl into. Then I felt honoured, you know, and chosen – it was terrific really, all mixed up with the nerves.' The mauve plastic disk suspended from one ear swung wildly as she shook her head at the memory.

'Go on,' said the Youngest Shepherd. 'You only wanted to be in it because of *me*.'

'It was you that wanted to be in it because of *me*,' protested Mary, giving him a push under the table where their knees and ankles were pressed close together.

'I sing of a maiden/That is makeles,' thought Tom, watching the flutter of Clare/Mary's plastic earring.

'You're both extremely good.' Humphrey

227

Hale was pacific. 'The whole thing gets better each time we do it, in spite of everything.'

'I don't know about it getting better – it changes,' Thomas sounded thoughtful. 'Even the first time – when we were all in a state of shock about poor Exelby – it all just came together, as if we really were medieval people celebrating their view of their world and their God. Each performance since has been different, but there's always something special, isn't there – something which comes off as it never has before.'

'Tell me then,' said Humphrey to Poison, 'when they told you you'd got the role, there wasn't much time to prepare, was there, when you had that concert tour right before?'

'I couldn't have done the gigs if I'd been thinking and preparing for this.'

'No, I see that.'

'Well – when I saw how people felt about it ... I was more shit-scared than ever ... nervous of offending people's feelings by seeming to show disrespect ... that's what everyone was expecting me to do, right?'

'Right,' said the Virgin Mary.

'Yeah,' said Thomas.

'I read the script for the first time my first day here and thought, "How the hell am I going to do justice to this?"'

'Having a Christian upbringing helps,' Humphrey meant to sound comfortable, comforting, understanding. He succeeded in sounding smug.

Poison's thin, bony fingers were fiddling compulsively with his glass, twirling it in jerks. The cubes of ice clattered sharply.

'Sure might have done if I'd had one.'

Everyone looked down at the table.

'Your family atheists then?' asked the Youngest Shepherd.

'If you'd asked me that at one time, I'd have said yeah, before I punched your teeth down your throat. I don't suppose they're anything. Never said anything about it to me.'

'Must have been worse being a pop star,' put in Clare. 'No experience of acting.'

'I don't agree,' Thomas said heatedly. 'What experience could anyone have brought to the role of Christ? However many RADAs they'd been to and however often they'd played the West End?'

Clare tossed her head and the Youngest Shepherd glared at Thomas. They both had their A levels lined up for the following year and he and Clare had both decided to try for Cambridge, before this damn fool talk of RADA had been started by Bruce Exelby. He had his life mapped out, and she was in it, and he didn't want any more upsets thank you.

'So you started level with everyone else then,' Humphrey said, interested enough to press on with the conversation in the face of antagonism. 'There could be no experience that was helpful with the spiritual aspect of this role.'

'S'right.'

'It seemed to me,' Thomas remarked, 'that you approached the role with a kind of reverent simplicity.'

'What else could I do? You just start in.'

'But if you don't mind me saying so, a kind of spirituality has entered your playing of it,' Humphrey was ignoring the young lovers, who were getting increasingly entwined beside him. His urbane sophisticated voice for once sounded deeply sincere, moved, even.

'Well, that's terrif.' Poison buried his nose in his glass and slurped. The dark lashes dropped over his golden-brown eyes. An air of embarrassed modesty and gratitude passed across him like the shadow of a cloud over a hillside.

Clare disentangled herself from the Youngest Shepherd. 'I've the same problems with my role,' she said perkily. 'But acting is a process of self-awareness, don't you think?'

'Awareness. Do we always have to put the emphasis on self?'

Thomas was irritated by her all of a sudden. Was it just that she was so sure of herself – so confident with the unseeing, selfish confidence and pampered youth? Whatever else he might be and do, Tom was sure Poison's childhood had been anything but pampered. When they were acting, Clare's youth, beauty and innocence brought a lovely radiance to her part; but Poison brought something else again – a growing majesty, spirituality and touching dignity; an authority and compassion, which the previous day had drawn tears from some of the audience. He had grown in stature immensely during the week's performances, startling enough though the first day's rendering had been.

'Don't know about you lot,' Poison rose, 'but I've got to get back. We've a play to put on, yeah?'

He walked out, stiff-legged. The detective who was trying to protect him got up hastily from another table and quietly followed him out.

Clare shoved the rest of her cheese and onion sandwich into her mouth and the Youngest Shepherd drained his beer. Humphrey, as always elegantly suited and immaculate, dusted a crumb from his long trouser leg. Thomas bundled himself to his feet, massively ignoring crumbs, which would not be seen anyway on his slightly hairy tweeds.

Poison was still standing on the edge of the pavement, though he was not looking round or in any obvious way waiting for them. They came up to him and surrounded him. A group united in common purpose, they walked across the road and back towards the Museum Gardens. A summer shimmer hung over everything. The river at the bottom of the road threw flashes of light into the air. A train thundered nearby on its way to Scarborough. The trees of the gardens leaned over the white limestone wall.

A girl in a white dress, looking Scandinavian with her blonde hair, singled out Thomas. 'Pliz tell me the way to ze Railway Museum?' she said. The group stopped. Thomas explained. 'And where is ze Museum Gardens?'

'Just here,' Thomas pointed and smiled. The others were growing impatient. The girl thanked Thomas with a dazzling smile and followed them into the Gardens.

They walked in past St Mary's Lodge where Bruce Exelby had had his flat, without glancing up.

The following day was the inquest.

10

Make room! Be alive! And let me gang
What makes here all this madding throng?
Hie you all hence! High might you hang,
 Right with a rope.
The Lokk Smyths' Play

The room was packed.

Reporters had come up from London,
having discovered from their experience of
the press conferences that they could be in
York in two hours by train and that once
there it was only ten minutes' walk to practically anywhere in the town centre. They
had looked around them at the crowds of
tourists, the warm sun on the ancient city
walls, the tree canopy over the dappled
Museum Gardens and along the river, and
found that there was life north of Watford,
and that it was good.

Outside the court room was a maze of
little spaces and passages, with several small
rooms used by magistrates, each furnished
with a carafe of water, a glass, and a blotter.
The reporters were jamming the court room
itself. Most of the cast had come along to
the court, as had production staff, ward-

robe, property, and front-of-house staff. Apart from those actually being called as witnesses most of them had not been able to get into the hearing. The result was that, together with a few members of the public, they were all milling about, passing on bits of information either correct or erroneous. It was easy enough for anyone to come in off the street, walk up the stairs, and lose themselves in that maze of small spaces...

The coroner took his place and the police began to produce their series of witnesses to the events of that night.

God was first – and recounted once again the events he had gone over so often.

Isaiah was next. He had been on stage, in Limbo, ready to join the conversation between Adam and Eve. Symeon, John the Baptist, and Moyses were waiting to walk forward and join in, each in turn. When Exelby climbed on to the stage Isaiah was about to speak. Exelby had stumbled past him, looking pale. Yes, the director had seemed to say something to him. It had sounded like a question, but he had only caught the last word of it. That was 'Father?' Yes, he was sure of it. Then the director had stumbled on and collapsed on to the stage. From then on he knew nothing more than anyone else.

After taking the evidence of Adam, Eve,

Symeon, John the Baptist, and Moyses, the coroner turned to Belzebub, Satan, and the little Devils.

They had been waiting in a group at Hell's Mouth, made like the mouth of a beast, with flames and dry-ice smoke. Where they were standing was rather dark. They burst out of it one by one a little later in the play, ran up the slope on to the stage, and there had a conversation with one another before the dramatic appearance of Jesus in the arch above. Only one of the Devils had been asked to appear at the inquest, to speak for all of them. He was the first on stage so he had been at the front of the group.

No, the play had not progressed far enough for him to come on stage. He had seen the director stumble across and fall, nothing else. After the police took charge they told the Devils they could go home, so they went back to the St Olave's parish room to change. Well, not straight away. Yes, they had stopped to talk to the Angels, who were waiting ready for the Mercers' Play, Doomsday. No, they hadn't realized the director was dead. To be honest they thought he was drunk and that it was all a bit amusing.

Then Sergeant Diamond gave his evidence, and next the coroner called the pathologist.

The death had been from a wound from a narrow-bladed knife of stiletto pattern, six to seven inches long. Yes, the knife produced by the police could have dealt the wound. The instrument had entered the chest wall at the level of the nipple on the left side and very slightly to the rear. It had passed through the left lung and made small punctures in both the left branch of the pulmonary artery and the aorta. These had caused bleeding into the left lung (from the pulmonary artery) and into the pleural cavity (from the aorta). This aortal bleeding had caused the collapse of the lung.

The victim would have experienced little pain at first. After fifteen to twenty seconds the loss of blood would lead to a rapid fall in the blood pressure, with shock, pallor, dizziness. About forty seconds after the blow he would begin to experience pain from the build-up of pressure in his left chest.

'My picture of what happened,' said the pathologist, 'is that he realized he had been attacked and might need help, that he climbed the ladder as the quickest way of reaching other people. By the time he stumbled past Isaiah he was dizzy and his breathing was becoming laboured; blood would be rising in his throat, making it difficult for him to speak more than a word or two. By the time he reached the position where he fell down he would be fainting. The sergeant tells us the pulse was rapid and weak.'

'Is it not surprising,' said the coroner, 'that

death did not take place within a few seconds?'

'The punctures in the arteries were small. I would say very small. Made virtually with the tip of a narrow knife. Had they been larger wounds death would have taken place in seconds.'

'Is it not surprising,' asked the coroner, 'that the wound did not bleed externally?'

'When a fine blade is withdrawn the puncture closes up. There was only a small stain of blood on the left side of the deceased's shirt, about an inch across.'

'If medical care had been available more quickly could Mr Exelby's life have been saved?'

'Impossible. He could not have survived a punctured aorta. Even in an intensive care unit. The blood loss is so rapid. Death from anoxia to the brain takes place within a couple of minutes.'

'Just over a couple of minutes in this case. Does that alter your diagnosis?'

'Not at all. The police tell me they have reconstructed his movements and timed them at two and a quarter minutes to two and a half. Bleeding in this case would be relatively slow. I stress, *relatively.*'

'Your postmortem revealed the wound?'

'It did. Also that the left side of the chest was full of clotted blood, with the lung completely collapsed.'

'Thank you.'

The police produced the weapon. It was six and a half inches long. It bore a trace of the victim's blood, which had been matched to his blood group. No fingerprints. No threads of fabric. Nothing else to aid them. The whole weapon had an antique and theatrical look. The presence of the initials B.E. on the handle was not mentioned.

It was in the press of people that Jane Bugg fainted.

'Give her some air,' commanded Sally Vause. 'Go and get some water to throw over her, somebody – there's some on the magistrates' tables. Be quick. Move back, everyone.' Clare, Susan Brown the assistant director, Velvet Smith the assistant wardrobe mistress, and Betty, Sandra, and Mrs Moore, members of MRS and of the Crowd, all went in search of water.

No one could move back. It was as much as they could do to make room for the six water-seekers to squeeze out.

'She isn't coming to at all. Anyone got a newspaper to fan her with? Lord, she is a lump. I can hardly shift her. Put some chairs together and let's lie her on those. She'll be better than on the floor where folks will tread on her. Why is there never a first-aider about when you want one?'

Several of the cast, not caring whether or

not Jane was trampled on but rallying to a certain extent to one of their number, heaved and strained to get her on to a line of hard upright chairs, where she lay uncomfortably, beginning to open her eyes and look around her. Clare brought a carafe of water. Sally administered it, by splashing it over Jane's face. Mrs Moore came with a bucketful, marked 'Fire'.

'Push her head in it,' someone suggested helpfully.

Velvet arrived a long time later with another carafe, and, finding it unwanted, drank some of the contents herself.

It was in the maze of small rooms and odd corridors, outside the courtroom, in a little empty room, that Tom, trying to find his way to a window for a breath of air, came across Sydney Absolom.

'You don't do yourself any good hanging about, Syd,' he said sternly.

'You don't understand, Tom.' Absolom grabbed Thomas by the lapel and hung on to him. 'I know who did it. I've been putting it all together in my head.'

Tom gently released Syd's grip on his jacket. It wasn't so much that he minded, but the jacket was linen, the only formal thing he could bear wearing on such a day as this, and it creased badly – even under a thin dry hand like Absolom's. Then he looked around. It seemed they were alone.

'You must go to the police. They'll find out quickly enough if you're right. Tell them what and who you suspect.'

'But they suspect *me*, Tom! How can I talk to them? They don't believe a word I say.'

'How can you be so sure that you know? What information have you got that the police haven't?'

'I've got better than information. I've got the knowledge of this city and its people over sixty-five years. The other day the way some-one was talking got me thinking, and I've remembered a lot of things – hidden things, Tom, that nearly everyone has forgotten, and when I say everyone, hardly anyone knew in the first place. Those few that did have an inkling have forgotten. I'd forgotten. But now I've remembered, and it's as plain as a pikestaff who's done it. You can't beat local knowledge. You think you know the city, Tom, but you've been here no time at all. You haven't shared in its miseries and triumphs, pleasures and pains like I have.'

'This is serious, Syd. You must go to the police.'

'Let me tell *you*. I don't want to go to the police. Let me tell you and you can decide then what the best action is for us to take.'

'You should have gone before, as soon as it came to you. Go now.'

'Don't start telling me what to do.'

'Syd, don't be touchy. I'm only thinking of what's best. You may be right and you may be wrong but the police are the people to deal with it. Don't worry. Don't bother your head about it. Keep calm. Stay away from the plays. Be sensible, Syd. Go and have a cup of tea, then tell the police all about it. Now *go*, there's a good chap.'

Tom paused, remembering his recurrent feeling of an evil undercurrent, hatred, assassination, death, murder. It all still seemed incredible. But he had just been inside that hot courtroom, testifying; Exelby had gone for ever; the evil was still at large. 'I don't see what good it will do to tell me.'

'It matters, Tom. To both of us.'

'You mean ... you mean it's someone we know ... it's practically bound to be, really, isn't it? Bound to be someone in the plays, or connected with them, I should think.'

'Someone you see every day at present, Tom.'

Tom shivered.

'Again, old chap, it's bound to be, isn't it? 'I expect I'm cowardly – I don't want to know who you suspect. You are probably wrong. That would bias me against that person and it wouldn't be fair. I'd rather the police sorted it out. You're playing with fire.'

Thomas didn't want to say that he had, nagging away at him, the feeling that he himself knew something significant – which

241

when it once came floating up into his consciousness, would unlock the riddle – he thought. He didn't want muddling up by anyone else's half-baked theories. He wanted to keep his mind clear for that thought to surface. It was hot and he was feeling fed up with his old friend Absolom.

'Go home, Syd,' he said again. 'I must get out of here for a breath of air. I think I'll go for a beer. Come if you want to.'

Without waiting to see if his friend was following him, Tom shouldered his way through the neighbouring room, which was packed, and through the tight knot of people at the head of the stairs. He clattered down the flight and out into the street, where a wave of dry hot air hit him. It might not be possible to fry an egg on the pavement but he thought it would have poached one lightly, if anyone had wanted to try.

Rapidly he turned left and found his way down the nearest street to the river. Once near the water there was cooler air, and he walked along to the pub at the end of King's Staith for a beer. Expecting Sydney to be following along behind him, in spite of his own brusqueness, he was surprised not to find him there when he looked round. Tom shrugged his shoulders and went in for his pint, then brought it out into the open and sat at one of the tables near the river. The place might not be perfect – it was overcrowded, and noisy with a hundred kids. But no one in sight was connected with the mystery plays, there was not a single policeman, and he didn't know a soul.

'Hello there,' said Linda. She took the seat opposite him, and Susan and Paul sat one on either side. 'What's a nice neighbour like you doing in a place like this?'

'I could ask you that.' He grinned with an effort. 'Can I treat you to anything?'

'We've got ours, thanks.' The barman had followed her out with a tray.

'I see you've got rid of that collar, Paul,' Thomas said to the boy.

'Didn't need that thing.'

'He's quite all right now. Probably we were a little over-cautious. I thought you were testifying today, Thomas?' said Linda, with a 'now-mind-your-manners' look at Paul.

'I've done my bit. Came out for a breath of air and a change. It will be over soon, I should think. I'll go back in five minutes and see what's happening.'

The police worked out afterwards that it must have been in the time of excitement just before the verdict was announced that Sydney Absolom fell from one of the second floor windows of the building, and split his skull on the pavement below.

People in Clifford Street on a hot June day in a festival week are mostly tourists on their way to and from the Castle Museum. Hardly any of them seemed to have even noticed the building housing the magistrates' courts on the other side of the street.

Some of them had noticed the sudden downward movement, as Sydney fell, out of the corner of their eyes, and turned their heads quickly enough to see the full impact of his head with the pavement. One of these people was immediately sick into the gutter.

The policeman on duty in the street, strolling up and down in his shirtsleeves, heard a shout and turned, running the few yards to where the man had smacked down. It was due to the policeman's presence of mind that the witnesses stayed where they were and didn't go rushing off to have a nice cup of tea and try to forget all about it. He yelled to them across the street, and those who thought they had seen what happened stayed where they were until another policeman arrived and took brief statements and their names and addresses.

The fact of seeing Absolom fall caused their imagination to conjure up earlier pictures of him standing at the window then leaning out, dangerously.

'Old men are daft, leaning out like that in the sun. Must have turned dizzy,' one of them said to his neighbour in the crowd. He was a burly, beer-bellied man with a small boy clinging on to his hand. The small boy was holding an ice-cream cornet in his free hand and licking it.

'I saw someone push 'im,' the small boy announced to all and sundry, not very clearly because of two missing front teeth and a mouthful of ice-cream. The roar of the traffic helped to drown his words, which made their way up to his father's ears as an irritating buzz.

'Shut up, Zen, or I'll thump yer,' said his father.

'I saw someone.'

'You didn't see nuthin'. Eat your ice-cream and shut up.'

A policeman approached. 'Did you see the accident, sir?'

'No,' said the man with the beer-belly.

'Thank you, sir. We won't detain you, then.'

The man and his child walked off in the direction of the Castle Museum.

'I saw someone push 'im, Dad.'

'You behave yourself or I'll tell your mam of you.'

The only witness to the crime was dragged off, protesting. To make it worse the ice-cream fell off the top of his cornet and landed irretrievably in the dust.

At the end of the hearing came the verdict. Murder by person or persons unknown. The door from the courtroom opened with difficulty, what with the people outside who wanted to get in and the people from inside who wanted to get out. The word spread, round the gradually opening door. The hearing was over, pending further inquiries. Murder by person or persons unknown. The words spread through the knots and groups of people in that maze of anterooms and corridors, among people who had not yet heard of the further death, outside.

There were no other witnesses. No one had noticed Sydney's presence at the court except Thomas Churchyard, and just when he might have been useful in keeping his friend company and preventing the fall, he must have been drinking beer, sitting in the sun on King's Staith and talking to Linda and the children, and assuming that Syd had gone home.

Everyone still in the magistrates' court building was detained there until they had given their names and addresses and had been questioned briefly by the police, which made them all hot and cross. No one had seen anything; it was obviously an accident; they were all very sorry about it and a little sickened by the details, but what good did it do keeping them here like this?

At last they were released, and by then time was very short before the evening performance. The cast and the backstage and front-of-house teams had to eat, rest, wash and change, and somehow arrive in time at the Museum Gardens.

'I suppose it was an accident,' said Bob Southwell thoughtfully.

'I've been in contact by phone with his doctor and he says the old chap had all kinds of things wrong with him and a fit of dizziness wouldn't surprise him at all, though he hadn't actually complained of it.'

'Good thinking. Thanks. Fix up the inquest, will you, Smart? We'll need a coroner's officer.'

'It will be very straightforward, sir. I could fit it in.'

'Right. Notify his relatives, and all that. I want a copy for myself of the list of people present in the magistrates' court and in the whole building at the time.'

Detective Inspector Smart nodded and went out of the incident post.

When Exelby was murdered Southwell had never had time to do any real detective work himself – the administration of his suddenly increased staff had fully occupied him. Now that the dust had settled he found his mind dwelling on the case.

It was the following afternoon that James Jester, who had asked to see the detective chief inspector, came into the murder room at the police station.

'How's the research going on, then?' asked Bob.

'Steadily, sir. Just found something interesting.'

The young detective was holding a piece of paper.

'Yes? What?'

Jester handed the paper over, saying as he did so, 'In an old theatrical periodical, sir.'

Bob looked at the photocopied photograph and its surrounding letterpress silently. It showed a young – a very young – Bruce Exelby, in Elizabethan costume. His profile was turned to the camera in the approved manner, and the paragraph underneath was headed, 'Promising young actor's debut as Hamlet.'

'I may be unusually stupid,' Bob said at last, 'but the significance of this escapes me.'

'But don't you see, sir? At his belt!'

Bob saw at once. The stiletto-type dagger thrust casually through the actor's belt was identical to the one which had more recently been thrust into his body. Holding the photocopy at an angle and peering at it closely, Bob thought he could pick out the slight gleam of the silver inlaid dots on the haft which spelt B.E. Certainly the whole elaborate shape was very familiar. James Jester shyly produced a magnifying glass and Bob looked through it. It didn't really help much but he did feel even more convinced that the tiny gleam was from the inlaid letters. He retuned the magnifying glass with an amused look.

'Do you always carry one of those?'

'Stamps are my hobby, sir.'

'I think you're right, Jester. That looks like our dagger. Which proves it was his own. When was this picture taken? I seem to remember that he wasn't an actor for long.'

'He wasn't, sir. It was taken here in York, at the Theatre Royal. He acted Hamlet while he was in the Rep – the resident repertory company.'

'So he had it when he was in York twenty years ago, but his secretary assures us she had never seen it among his possessions at his flat. Suggestive, eh?'

'Yes, sir.'

'It might be as well to check all the later photographs you can before we jump to any conclusions.'

'Yes, sir.'

'Like, if he left the dagger behind in York – it was here all the time – and he came back to join it…'

'I'll do some more checking, sir.'

'I've remembered something,' Bob Southwell said. 'It might be anything or nothing. My next-door neighbour once told me that in his pet society (he's a great one for these voluntary organizations) only three members had been born in York. He's on holiday and will probably be in his garden at this time of day. Just have a trip out and ask him to tell you how long each member of his society have lived in the city – to the best of his knowledge. The three who were born here might be of no significance if some of the others have been here for over twenty years ... assuming Exelby's former residence in the city is of any relevance... Just take down what Mr Churchyard can tell you from memory, we can check out more detail later.'

Jester came back within the hour with a list. The three who had been born in York were Sydney Absolom, Sally Vause, and Velvet Smith. Thomas himself had lived in the place eleven years; George Grindal he believed about five; Mr and Mrs Moore had retired to the city a couple of years before; the newsletter editor was married to an official in a bank who moved their executive staff regularly, and so had probably only been resident a few years; the university student was a bird of passage; and Betty and Sandra Tweddle had come from the Malton area when they opened their flower shop, which event Tom Churchyard remembered, so that must be less than eleven years ago.

'Right, Jester.' Bob Southwell looked pleased, and thoughtful. 'Now fetch me that list of people present in the magistrates' courts building yesterday.'

All of MRS had been, at one time or another – for Tom had left before the name-taking – except George Grindal, who had more urgent matters to attend to in the shape of saving someone from their urge to end it all.

There was really no need for Thomas to be involved any further in the affairs of his old friend Sydney Absolom. He was depressed and blaming himself enough without any addition to his mood. But the next day a telephone call involved him – a call from Sydney's sister, Mrs Baines, who had travelled from Wilberfoss where she was living out a retired widowhood. She wanted his help in clearing things up, and Thomas could not refuse her.

Once more he arrived at the neat little house in the inner suburbs, and walked up the concrete path from the gate, the concrete marked out to imitate crazy paving. Mrs Baines opened the door to him. She was wearing a hat, and in the next few days when Thomas saw quite a lot of her he never saw her without one, so he could not have said whether the puffs of white hair which were so characteristic of Sydney were also sported by his sister. A few grey-white curls around the edge of the hat made him think they might be, and he looked rather wistfully at them.

She shook his hand firmly, and insisted that he drank a cup of tea. At least that had not changed. It was just as thick and dark as in Sydney's time, and served in the same cup with rampant roses. It seemed strange that the cup should still be there when its owner was lying in the mortuary.

'He never had dizzy spells,' was Mrs Baines's opening fusillade.

'He didn't mention them to me, no.'

'Because he didn't have them. I know what he had.' Mrs Baines embarked on a recital of Sydney's physical ailments, concluding: 'But he didn't have dizzy spells. Marvellous on heights our Sydney was. I've seen him walking on our roof many a time. He used to like getting up there when father checked it over once a year. He always cleaned out the gutters and did the bedroom windows. Loved being up a ladder, our Sydney did.'

'That doesn't mean he would never have dizzy spells, Mrs Baines. He was getting older, you know.'

'He were two years younger than me.' Mrs Baines was very positive in her tones whatever she said. 'And look at me! I'm all right!'

'But you've just been telling me how many things he had wrong with him.'

'Yes. But nothing *serious.*'

'What are you trying to tell me?'

'That someone pushed our Sydney. He would never have fallen out of a window on his own. But if he'd been looking out, someone could have pushed him.'

'We all get old, Mrs Baines, and old people on very hot days do tend to get dizzy.' Tom had the feeling that he was going round and round in this argument just as he had on occasions with Sydney.

'He was murdered,' Mrs Baines stated impressively.

'You had better tell the police what you think.' This was familiar too. Tom shuddered.

The inquest was held quickly on Sydney Absolom. The medical evidence was clear on the cause of death. There seemed to be no basis for a verdict of anything except accidental death. There was very little evidence of any kind. The hearing was soon over, the funeral soon arranged, and Thomas stood at the graveside of his old friend.

But it was not only in Mrs Baines's mind that a doubt remained. Thomas, talking to Bob Southwell in their back gardens, mentioned not only her conviction that her brother was particularly good with heights, but also his own conversation with the dead man, in which he had tried to persuade Sydney to tell his suspicions to the police.

'It was all very vague,' he explained. 'I'm afraid I wouldn't listen.'

'We all regret something, after a death,' Bob said with sympathy. 'Errors of commission

253

and omission. The only positive thing we can say is that it makes it look very doubtful that he was the murderer of Exelby.'

'I've always been sure that he was not.'

'And off the record I agree with you. Apart from anything else, Smart went to see Mrs Baines – it is part of the coroner's officer's duties to contact the relatives and do all he can. She told him that Absolom thought he had discovered the murderer – so you were not the only one he confided in.'

'Yes, I know he had told Mrs Baines.'

'You didn't say so to me.'

'Well … I didn't think it significant…'

'It is very significant, Tom. The fact that you were not the only person he confided in is very significant.'

'You would expect him to tell his sister, if he saw her – they didn't meet that often, but they were close.'

'And she would have known the people he knew, twenty years ago or longer.'

'Yes, she would have.'

'So he may have told her more than he told you, in a crowded building when you were being rather impatient with him.'

'Yes.'

'Absolom, because of his long residence in the city, had special knowledge, and he had used it to make a deduction. That means that the person he believed to be the murderer had most likely also lived here twenty years ago, when Exelby was a young actor at the Theatre Royal. It was something that Absolom remembered from those days which, he felt, gave a motive.'

'I see that; but I did tell you he thought he knew who did it.'

'But as well as telling you, he also told his sister. He may have told a hundred people. He may have told the person he suspected, perhaps in order to get them to own up.'

'He said it was someone I knew well, and saw every day.'

'Who do you see every day?'

'I see Jane Bugg for one, and often wish I didn't. She's a clerical assistant in our office.'

'Jane Bugg told me that Syd committed suicide by leaping from the window, because he really had murdered Exelby.'

'Always helpful, our Jane,' said Tom bitterly. 'She's like that at work. Always sure she knows best, and she's usually wrong. I don't know why they keep her, except that she puts on a good front and bluffs her way out of everything.'

'So you think she did the murder?'

'No, I don't. It doesn't seem in character, somehow.'

'She did faint – wouldn't that be a sign of guilt?'

'Are you postulating that Syd was murdered also? She couldn't have done that while she was fainting.'

'Just before?'

'I don't know,' said Tom wearily.

But Bob knew that Jane had been in a small room with several other people just before she fainted, and if anyone was responsible for Sydney's fall it was unlikely to be her, and the reason for her faint was more probably heat than guilt. It was fairly certain that she had been unconscious when the accident occurred. He moved on to another tack.

'Is there anyone else you see every day?'

'Now I come to think of it, Sydney said "every day at present". That's different to normal days.'

'Mrs Baines told Smart that Syd had known one of MRS long before, that the person was embezzling money from the firm they both worked for, and that he let her – yes, it was a her – know that he knew, to stop the proceedings; but he didn't give her away to the bosses, because she did stop doing it.'

'That could only be...'

'Velvet Smith?'

'Either Velvet or Sally Vause. But Velvet is our treasurer and absolutely spot on, and Sally was head of an important office dealing with money all the time.'

'Smart put the same point to Mrs Baines.'

'And?'

'Apparently she said, "Other times, other manners."'

256

'A bit of embezzling in youth is hardly the same as murder in middle age...'

'True. It probably is of no significance whatever, only telling us that we should have approached Mr Absolom from quite a different angle, and quizzed him in a friendly way over his memories.'

'Is that what you've been doing to me? "Quizzing in a friendly way"? I feel as if I'd been put through the third degree,' Tom said ruefully, looking over the shrubs.

'I'm sorry, Tom. But I am a policeman, as well as a friend, and you want me to find the murderer as much as I want to find him. And stop worrying about your friend Sydney – you aren't responsible for his death.'

'Did Mrs Baines tell you who exactly it was Syd suspected?'

'No. In the end he turned coy and didn't name the name.'

Tom went off comforted, but Bob found himself brooding on the conversation. Was Absolom's death a second murder? As the days went by he became gradually convinced – by something within himself rather than by evidence – that it was.

11

Now see I sign of solace clear,
A glorious gleam to make us glad.

The Saddlers' Play

Once more Thomas Churchyard and Poison
Peters were sitting on the grass in the
Museum Gardens. Tom had been to Miller's
Yard on Gillygate and bought filled rolls of
wholemeal bread and a few other things for
their lunch. Tourists and peacocks strolled
about the Gardens.

In their protective coloration of casual
clothes (including Poison's 'Erik Blood-Axe
Rules OK' T-shirt) they went unnoticed.
Poison swigged quite openly from his bottle
of Malvern water. Talking quietly, they felt
as secure from scrutiny as they would have
done in Poison's caravan, and the dappled
grass, the rose beds, the varied trees, the
general atmosphere of holiday, relaxed them
much more than being shut in a small
space.

They could even forget the presence of
Poison's protective detective, who sat at a
little distance with his eyes scanning the
crowd for assassins. The only ones he saw

were the peacocks, who now and then attacked those tourists who were eating buns, with the idea of getting their share.

One of them came up to Poison, who threw him some scraps of bread. The peacock gobbled them down then shrieked for more, opening its unlovely mouth and emitting a noise like a furious tom cat.

'They won't even spread their tails for it,' commented Tom.

'Food just for shouting. Maybe that's what I get, food for shouting.'

'I think they're rather ugly birds, dragging their worn-out tattered feathers behind them, and look at those scaly legs.'

For a while they watched the peacock silently, until it stalked off.

'Tell me,' said Tom, 'What made the difference? You told us once about how terrified you were at the idea of playing the part. What made the difference? How did you come to realize how to tackle the job?' As he asked he felt uncomfortably that these were the very kind of questions the media people asked Poison and how sick he must be of it.

'It was funny.' Poison was gazing upward into the blue air over the trees. 'I was in a fix. We had a party to celebrate my casting, did I tell you that? Bruce Exelby threw it. Showbiz people, you know, and press, all the shower. Champers, caviare, congrats, the works. Finished at two in the morning. I was legless by then.'

'On spring water?'

'Potent stuff, yeah? Anyway they sent for the hire car I use in London and carried me down and put me into it. I always have the same driver. He knows my habits. They keep him on contract for me and I pay through the nose. He drove me home, I changed, then he took me down by the river. I wanted a walk, think things out, see?'

'Still worried?'

'Yeah. So I went on one of my night prowls you don't approve of.'

'In present circumstances it's dangerous,' said Tom under his breath.

'Usually it helps. But this time I was just as miserable and shit-scared as ever. Then I dropped into this caff, after I'd walked for a bit, early morning; and I mean caff – a right dump – down and outs go there – and sat down at the same table as this old geezer. Dog collar. Ugly sort of bloke. Looked as if someone had squashed his face in. Not the sort you gaze at with joy, know what I mean?'

'What was he doing in a place like that? Dog collar? Was he one of the down and outs?'

'No, not him. You do get vicars in them sort of places sometimes.'

'Go on.'

'We started talking. D'ya know, he had a beautiful voice. It was strange, coming out of that ugly mug. The sort of voice that doesn't operate in single notes. The sounds are more like chords. Know what I mean?'

'I think so. I'm not as musical as you of course.'

'Huh!' Poison was diverted from his topic for a minute. 'What about all that egg-head stuff on disc, then?'

'That's for listening. What I mean is – that's my hobby or one of them – music's your craft. The ways of looking at sounds are different.'

'Yep.' In a second, Poison had comprehended, agreed, filed away all the subtleties of the remark, and returned to the previous discussion. 'Like I said, we started talking. Somehow I found myself telling him about it – asking his advice if you like, though not in as many words. I told him all sorts of things, come to think of it, that I've never told anybody else. He was that kind of man. If I hadn't met him then I might have chucked the whole thing in.'

'He helped?'

'Right. Just read Luke, he said. Read the Gospel of St Luke and try to feel it, to imagine it, to take it into yourself. That's all the preparation you need do now. Leave the rest until the time comes. Then when he got up to go he stood and looked down at me a minute, then put his hand on my sleeve, friendly-like. "God bless the work," he said. Boy, he was an ugly bastard.'

'Sounds like George.' Thomas was thoughtful.

'You what?'

'It sounds to me as though you met one of our Canons from the Minster, George Grindal. You've described him very well.'

'You mean you know him? He lives here in York?'

'I think he's your man. He lives here, but he's away a lot, various work he does. He's away now. He's a member of my society, MRS. It's typical of him to be in a sleazy caff for down-and-outs in the middle of the night in London. And he was present when we were discussing your appointment, and never said a word – and he knew you, and how you felt, all the time.'

'I thought all you MRS people were in the plays? I've never seen him.'

'No. He is involved, we're all involved. But what he does is advise on the text if they need someone who knows the original and can read it. Exelby wanted a few changes and George helped sort them out so that they were authentic. But that was before you arrived.'

'I'd like to meet him again,' said Poison. 'Tol tell him it all worked out. And to thank him. I said to myself over and over, "Just read Luke.'"

'Oh, it worked out all right. It certainly worked out.'

Worked out it had.

The plays were the biggest success ever (though on one level or another, someone said that of every production). As the time went by and the cast stood on the edge of their third week, the success took them and the whole city, lifting them high above normal life and expectations, producing one of those idyllic periods of seven days when life is transcended. And this, even though the shadow of the unsolved murder still hung over them.

'PETERS TRIUMPHANT' screamed the headlines and the placards propped up next to the street-corner newspaper sellers, by the Guildhall, in Exhibition Square, and in Rougier Street.

'EXELBY'S CASTING VINDICATED.'
'POP STAR WINS THROUGH.'
'MYSTERIES BREAK ALL RECORDS.'

The week began – as good weeks do – with Sunday, and the Sunday papers, and Thomas Churchyard read the *Sunday Times* over breakfast. He always had bacon and egg for breakfast on Sunday. When he got to the play reviews he was startled to see large photographs of the mystery-play production all over the top of the page. It was obvious that their fame had spread country-wide. Whether or not because the attention of the national press had been caught by the murder Thomas did not wait to find out. He wanted to share this with someone, and while he had been cooking he had noticed that Linda was out in the back garden next door. Remembering that he had shaved, reassured that he was tidy enough to be seen, he dashed out of his back door.

'Look at this!' he exclaimed. 'Fame at last!'

Linda was planting out annuals from a polystyrene punnet. The children had erected a tent on the lawn (which under their onslaught was rapidly turning into grass) and were both inside it, visible only as an occasional limb projecting under the canvas. Linda rocked back on her heels and looked up at Thomas.

'That looks good,' she said. 'Read it to me.'

As Thomas read Linda got to her feet and stood listening, trowel in hand.

'"The quality of the York mystery plays is superb this year,"' he read. '"The evocative and surpassingly beautiful set, part modern reconstruction and part ancient ruins, and the quality of the open-air setting in perfect weather, would certainly help any production; but this production needs no help.

It would function in a village hall. Bruce Exelby's swan song – as it unfortunately has turned out to be – is a crown worthy of his previous career. The costumes"' – and here he had a long paragraph to read, discussing the design of the costumes, which Tom found tedious, but Linda looked interested – '"and now, first in importance, we turn to the acting. Against all predictions Mr Poison Peters has proved that he is an actor of outstanding quality. His rendering of the role of Christ, one of the most difficult in the theatre, is such as we are not likely to see again for a long while. Anyone privileged to be present at one of the performances is likely to remember it for the rest of their lives as an outstanding theatrical and religious event. As the only professional actor in a cast of amateurs he might have been badly supported, but such is not the case. Thomas Churchyard as God" … er humph … yes…' Thomas stopped reading abruptly.

'Go on,' said Linda.

'There's a bit here might interest you,' said Thomas. 'Clare has got a good write-up for her Virgin Mary.'

'Never mind the Virgin Mary,' said Linda. 'What does it say about God?'

Thomas pretended he hadn't heard her. '"The sheep gave a remarkable air of verisimilitude,"' he read. '"Contrary to reports that their discipline had caused trouble to the production, their behaviour was impecc-able.'"

'Blow the sheep,' said Linda, and, catching him unawares, twitched the newspaper from his hand, and moved further away quickly so that he couldn't easily snatch it back again.

'It's an honour to get a write-up in the *Sunday Times*. Now let's see. "Thomas Churchyard as God was also outstanding. He is a fine and impressive actor and no professional could have brought out more dignity and presence. The human foibles so touchingly represented by the Crowd con-trasted splendidly with the acting of Christ and God, who were well supported by Michael, Gabriel, and the cast of Angels." Well! There's glory for you!'

'Quite,' said Tom. 'I hadn't actually read that bit or I don't think I would have rushed out here with it like that.' He felt embar-rassed, exhilarated and excited.

Linda smiled mischievously at him. 'Go on. Enjoy your fame. Why not? We all get knocked enough in this world. Let's have a sherry to celebrate. Stay there. Don't you dare go away.'

Tom rather liked being ordered about by Linda. He stood obediently where he was while she darted off. The sun shone, and the children in the green cool of the tent were playing a card game. Their high voices raised in dispute enhanced rather than spoiled the special atmosphere of a sleepy sunny Sunday morning. He decided that it was pleasant to have this young family next door to him. Not that they were that young. He thought Bob Southwell was about his own age, but Linda was a few years younger. He couldn't imagine Mrs Spartan who used to live there commanding him to stay still while she brought sherry out into the garden.

'By the way, where's Bob?' he asked, as Linda reappeared with a tray, bottle, and glasses.

'Working and worrying as usual over your wretched murder,' she said. 'I was hoping he might arrive to join us. Perhaps he will. He went in to the murder room early and promised to be back in an hour. It's two hours already so he's about due. I brought three glasses.'

'Mum! Can we have some? Mum!'

'No you jolly well can't. You can go and get the lemonade bottle and some biscuits and picnic in the tent.'

'Oh great!' There was a stampede from the tent followed before Linda had finished pouring sherry by a boisterous return and a dive into the low ark of canvas. 'Can we eat our dinner in here as well, Mum? Mum!'

'Perhaps,' answered Linda. 'Look, Tom, will you do something for me?'

'Yes, what?'

'Bob's getting all worked up over this case. Can you do anything to help him unwind?'

Tom did not know what to say at first. 'Isn't he used to things like this investigation?' he asked tentatively.

'Yes, of course he is up to a point. But – it might surprise you to know that policemen are people – they can still find murder investigation upsetting – when one human being hates another enough to inflict this kind of violence. And apart from anything like that, Bob's just been promoted – new area – changed houses – he can't move for media people – there are plenty of strains in the situation.'

'I can see there must be … journalists have been after me too, asking questions and wanting interviews … I wonder what I can do… Does he fish? I've got a good collection of records of classical music – any good? Does he play chess?'

'Oh, Tom. Don't you ever do just ordinary things? Like going to the pub?'

'Of course I do. This is very excellent sherry, Mrs Southwell. Your good health.'

'Here's Bob. Darling, come and join us. We're celebrating a super write-up of the plays in the *Sunday Times*.'

As Bob came towards them with his light stride Tom found himself agreeing with Linda that there was an appearance of strain around the eyes and mouth. But Bob kept all weariness out of his voice as he reached for a glass.

'How civilized! Sherry in the garden on Sunday morning.'

'Let's be even more civilized,' Tom answered, 'and go for a pint before Sunday lunch. You haven't made the acquaintance of our local yet.'

'You mean I'll have to come and haul you out when the Yorkshire puddings are ready?' cried Linda in mock horror.

'Do you think anything could make me late for my Yorkshires?' teased Bob, but Linda knew only too well that a good many things could come between him and proper nourishment at regular times, so she only pouted in reply, grateful that Tom had responded so quickly to her request.

Bob and Tom went to the Greyhound. In the dark cluttered interior no one turned round to look at them or jumped at them with a tape recorder. There was an atmosphere of busy relaxation. They leaned on the bar. 'Two pints of bitter please,' Tom said. 'OK for you, Bob? It's real ale.'

'Great.'

The landlady greeted Thomas as an old friend. He joked with her over the bar counter. After the beer was served they moved over to a small table where they could catch a glimpse of the green outside and a couple of tethered horses.

'You a regular here?' asked Bob, visibly relaxing.

'He's been all sorts,' put in the landlady, who had followed them over so that she could wipe a table which had just been left empty. 'Helped me behind the bar – chucked people out–'

'You haven't, have you, Thomas?'

'If Tom chucks someone out they stay chucked out,' confirmed the landlady.

Tom buried his nose modestly in his beer.

'She makes the best onion sandwiches in York,' he confided to Bob. 'A friend of mine – he's often in here, too, but I can't see him today – is fond of onion sandwiches and has got her trained.'

'I don't think I'll go in for them; Linda might object.'

'Oh well, this pal of mine isn't married.'

'About this murder–' said Bob.

'Don't you ever think of anything else?'

'Not until it's sorted out, no. Some extra Crowd costumes were made, weren't they? Task Force used them. Couldn't anyone who wanted to murder Exelby have got hold of one and mingled with the Crowd?'

'Yes, I suppose that's possible. But the wardrobe people would have noticed, surely.'

'There are a lot in the cast...'

'It's possible. Now, let's have a game of dominoes.'

Bob agreed, thinking to himself that the

Crowd did not wear gloves, and if the chance of a Devil's costume had come up, that would have been even better. Then he really did relax, and played dominoes.

One of the strange things about his role, Poison found, was that fans, when they managed to get through to him, did not want to sleep with him but to ask his advice on their problems.

He seemed to be expected to know everything and be able to help them on everything. It was humbling. The look in the eyes which beseeched help did not make him puffed up but brought home to him how little he or anyone could mitigate human suffering. Those people whose small problems filled their sky seemed just as much in need of help as those whose problems were so immense that only God himself could have made any difference to them.

Poison did his best. It was a small best, for he had no power to alleviate anyone's troubles. But to himself, as so often before in the last few weeks, he said, 'Read Luke,' and something out of his reading might come into his head and give some comfort to the other person.

Tom had told him that George Grindal had returned to York and was looking forward to meeting Poison again; and they went together to the Minster.

As they entered at the west door a young Scandinavian tourist came rushing up to them. She was blonde, dressed in a pure pale-yellow dress drawn in round her narrow waist, and Tom braced himself to tell her the way to somewhere. But for once she took no notice of him. Her blue eyes were all for Poison Peters.

'Will you write on ze book?' she asked, and, without drawing breath, went on, 'And the such a funny name, is it fish?'

'Is what fish?' asked Peters.

'Zis Poisson. Is the French for fish, yes?'

'Poisson is the French for fish. But my name's Poison, gedit?' he answered, but she obviously did not understand him. He sighed elaborately and took the paper she held out, which was a programme for the mystery plays. Thomas handed him a ballpoint.

'I've written "Poisson" now, with her saying it,' Peters remarked to Tom. But he turned back to the paper, lifted the pen and on the programme's white border drew the outline of a simple fish, with a sudden concentration, as though it was a symbolic act.

Returning the programme to the girl, he gave her a radiant smile; catching up with Tom, he looked as though freed from a burden; his back was straight and tall; he moved smoothly as though swimming. Tom looked at him out of the corner of his eye, but

273

Poison was rapt and silent. The vast sacred cool creaminess of the long airy vaulted space absorbed them. The presence of many other visitors did not disturb them. They moved slowly up the length of the nave aisle.

As they came level with the choir Julia Bransby came rapidly across their path, looking bright and alive.

'What are you doing here?' asked Tom.

'Oh, hello, Tom, congrats on the success! I've just been having a look at an altar frontal. They wanted to discuss conservation. Thank goodness people are getting more conscious all the time about the need to preserve things. There's the most smashing stuff here. My favourite's relatively modern though – an embroidered hanging from the Versailles of Marie Antoinette. Incongruous, perhaps, but so lovely. Found like so many of the beautiful textiles in the Minster by Dean Milner White. This altar frontal I've just been to see isn't nearly so glamorous. But interesting, of course.'

She paused for breath and smiled at Peters.

'We've come to see George Grindal.'

'But I've just left him! He's gone to the vestment room I think.'

They went back with her to the low arched door, where she parted from them. Thomas following her with his eyes.

'Does she always talk ten to the dozen like that?'

'Not usually. She's rather quiet as a rule, but something's excited her.'

'Fancy her, do you?' asked Poison.

'I do rather.'

Thomas knocked lightly, then opened the door. George had his back to them, and was putting an ancient rose-red Portuguese cope, half as old as time, away in the wide drawers.

'Look – I'll leave you,' Tom said suddenly. 'You don't need me. I'll dash after Julia and ask her if she's time to have a coffee with me in the Dean Court. You'll know where to find us for the next half hour. If not, I'll see you tonight.'

'Right.'

Poison went in alone to meet George Grindal again. The detective stood outside the closed door. The two voices in conversation were very faintly audible through its thickness. The man could distinguish no words until half an hour later when the door swung open again.

'There's someone who would like to meet you,' George said as the two of them emerged from the vestment room. 'Are you free for the next hour?'

'Yes.' Poison looked serene. For George he was willing to do a great deal.

'I'll just ring and see if it's convenient. If so we'll go now.'

A few minutes later they were picked up

(complete with detective) from the west door of the Minster by a long black limousine.

'So pleased to have the chance to meet you, Mr Peters,' said a tall elderly man coming forward to take his hands. 'In our Christian work it is not often we have the assistance of someone like yourself. Your influence with young people – I may say, with people of all ages, in your role as Christ – is now doing great good.'

For once Poison was speechless. The dwelling had an overwhelming aura of graciousness and sanctity. He had never been in a palace before, even a relatively small one, nor spoken with one of the heads of the Church. He longed to look round the room – gaining a better picture to remember of vast oil paintings and polished dark wood, and windows looking out on to lawns and flowers. But he could not break away from the forcefield generated by the archbishop.

'Thank you, your Grace,' he said at last.

'Do sit,' the tall man released Poison's hands and sat down himself in a comfortable chair. Poison sat near him, George Grindal taking a place nearer the door.

'Tell me, Mr Peters, what has given you this spiritual power which you are exerting so well?'

'I feel as if I'm only trying – not achieving–'

'You are achieving. Yes indeed. Have you always been a believer?'

'Well, no, your Grace. My mother was, but she died when I was six. My stepmother doesn't believe in anything much, nor does my dad. But–' and the pop star was emboldened by the other's close attention. If he was ever to speak of these things, it must be now. 'I think the worship of God is basic in mankind. If you hear about the earliest men, they revered something and worshipped something. It is necessary for men to do that. It's in us, somehow. There's another thing. Even the worst of men knows right from wrong. If they chose to do wrong they know they are doing it. This difference of right from wrong isn't taught to us necessarily, it's in us. I don't go to church. But I can't help feeling that there's something somewhere that's good, and that I want to look up to, and noticing that however bad people are, they know that they're being bad – they know there's a difference. Yeah?'

'Yes. It's taken some of our best thinkers a lifetime to see that as clearly as you have done, Mr Peters.'

They talked for some time. At last, venturing on remonstrance: 'Then tell me … why do you do wrong things in your life? It does worry me that you, thinking as you do, should ever set a bad example to our young people.'

'Well it's what they expect, see – it's not really like that, your Grace.'

'You don't take drugs?'

'No way.'

'But don't you think it harms all these young women – groupies, don't you call them – to encourage them to be promiscuous–?'

Poison went dull red. 'I'm not that keen on them, actually...'

The archbishop hastily dropped the subject. He showed Poison round the gardens, drowsy in the summer sun and yet alive with the sound of bees, and they parted at the end of half an hour the best of friends.

'Do you know,' the archbishop said thoughtfully some time afterwards, when talking this encounter over with George Grindal, 'I am tempted to believe that boy is, as they used to say, ha-ha, er, a' – here he looked embarrassed – 'well, a "clene maiden"? It may seem incredible to you but it was borne in upon me that he was altogether a remarkably pure young man ... quite impossible of course, don't you think?'

It was an hour after leaving the Minster that the long Limousine deposited Poison, George and detective back in the centre of York.

It had been quite involuntary that first time, when in giving his autograph, Poison had written Poisson and added the fish; having done it once, he did it again; and then one day, instead of a signature, he drew only the sign of the fish.

He looked at it in surprise and thought that he ought to try to get more sleep. Every night he had been keeping vigil, praying for help and guidance, and by degrees the vigils had been getting longer. If his body was starting to play tricks on him he had better try for eight hours. He was sustained by adrenalin, upheld by ecstasy.

Bob Southwell had returned to the statements which had been collected so painstakingly by his briefly enlarged team in the few heady days straight after the murder of Bruce Exelby. He had had them all printed out by the computer; the printouts had all extraneous matter cut away so that they read simply and clearly. He thought he had hit on a discrepancy.

'Jester,' he shouted.

'Yes, sir?'

'Do you remember how many Devils there are in the mystery plays?'

'There doesn't seem to be a set number, sir, but this time they appointed seven, only one got the sack if you recall, sir, and so there are six.'

'I certainly thought so. I have six dots for them, here on my plan on the stage – waiting outside the mouth of Hell in the darkness before bursting through the dry-ice smoke and up the slope.'

'That's right, sir.'

'But here we have a statement – from one of the Task Force, no less – that when Sergeant Diamond thought Exelby had been taken ill, and told him to "get that lot out of here," he sent the seven little Devils home. I've looked through all the other statements. Lots of them mention the Devils, but it is only David Longman who gives a number.'

'In the heat of the moment would he pause to count?'

'Counting is an odd thing, Jester. Do you ever play a game which involves dice?'

'I have done, sir.'

'And when you shake out the dice, do you count every spot?'

'No.'

'No – because they form a pattern, and you notice the pattern. You don't mistake three dots for four dots, even without counting.'

'But the Devils wouldn't be standing in regular rows, or anything like that.'

'True, and it was growing dark. But people instinctively recognize a pattern, and, I think, if things are odd or even. Get a message out to that member of Task Force and ask him to come in, now, this minute.'

Bob busied himself with some sheets of scrap paper and one or two felt-tip pens.

'They looked just like they always had,' the

man from Task Force said later. 'Just a group of lads in red and black, with those helmets on. Really weird. You could almost believe they were devils.'

'Perhaps one of them was.'

The policeman looked at his superior with a doubtful expression. Was he going round the twist? Did he mean that a real devil from Hell was among the group in costume?

'Many people in the outer office, Longman?' asked Southwell conversationally.

'About six, sir.'

'How many steps on your staircase at home?'

'Twelve.' By now Longman was convinced his superior was going crackers.

'How many miles on the clock in your car?'

'8,645.'

'New, is it?'

'New last year, sir.'

Southwell took the sheets of paper he had been doodling on. 'Now look at this, Longman. I'm going to show you these quickly and I want you to tell me how many dots there are without actually going, "one, two, three". Don't pause for thought.'

They were all irregular groups of dots. Like a teacher with flash-cards and a small child, Bob showed them to Dave Longman. The man from Task Force smartly spoke out numbers, quickly and without thinking, as he had been instructed. He had to be quick to keep pace as Bob Southwell rapidly changed the sheets.

'Well, Jester?' asked Bob when he had been through them all twice.

Jester had been ticking off the numbers as Longman spoke them. Southwell had written a list in advance, in the order in which he intended to show them.

'They are all right, sir, bar one.'

The one Dave had got wrong was a group of twelve; with all the lesser numbers he had been spot on.

'Now you try, Jester. Longman, write down what he says.'

James Jester was not as accurate as David Longman, but got the majority right.

Bob Southwell drew in a long breath. 'Dave, you're one of those people who can't help noticing the numbers of things in your environment. Lads, let's celebrate. Fetch your coffee in here and we'll add something medicinal. Just this once. I think we've cracked it.'

'You mean...'

'There was a Devil too many.'

Walking quietly along the narrow lane called Almery, Southwell came in sight of the low one-storeyed St Olave's parish room, scene of many a romp, what with bring-and-buys and charity book sales and Sunday School Christmas parties and auctions by reputable auction houses, and the wardrobe of the mystery plays.

He found a place where the wall not too far away took a step backward into somebody's garden, making a little dog-leg of itself, and drew in there, resting unobtrusively. For a while he watched the random comings and goings of cast and wardrobe and property staff. At last the activity died down. Then he left his convenient niche and went up to the wooden door and pushed it open.

'Anybody at home?' he called genially.

'Hello, detective chief inspector,' said Sally Vause.

'Mind if I come in?'

'Please do. Although I'm just off. All packed up for the night.'

Sally was alone, and looking tired.

'Just thought I'd have a look round.'

The costumes hung neatly around the space. Bob drifted about, touching one here and there, with no apparent purpose. At last he came to the row of seven Devils' costumes, each with its helmet mask in front of it on the floor.

'Do they each have their own?' he asked.

'Yes. We started by making seven basic costumes, but when the boys actually came, we altered them a little to fit.'

'Bit small for me!'

Sally thought the detective chief inspector very witty.

'My son Paul would love to try one on,' he said. 'I don't suppose I could borrow one, just overnight?'

'Well…'

'There's one you aren't using, isn't there? The boy who played that silly practical joke?'

'Oh, that's the biggest.' Sally pointed to it, at the end of the row. 'We had to let that out a bit instead of taking it in. Yes, you could borrow that one overnight with pleasure, as long as I get it back first thing tomorrow. It might be wanted as a spare if one of the others gets torn or something. I don't know how we've managed so far without any accidents of that kind.'

'What time will you be here?'

'I open up at ten. Silly really, I needn't until tea-time. But it's amazing how often there's a job. And I'm retired, so why not be here in case I'm needed?'

'Why not, indeed.'

Southwell had, as she was talking, lifted up first one and then another of the arms of the Devil costumes. In the dim light she could not be sure what he was doing – he seemed to be almost stroking the fabric of the hand coverings. It was surprising that a man should take such an interest – women often handled the costumes for the sheer pleasure of touching them, but men usually pretended to be above such things.

'This is the spare, then?' He had lifted

284

down the one she had indicated and was rolling it up carefully.

Sally would rather have rolled it up herself, but she did not protest.

'Goodnight – and many thanks. You will have made one little boy very happy.'

But Bob Southwell did not drive off towards home. His car was parked conveniently near the parish room, on the car park which stretched over the place where once several little streets of terrace houses had been home to hundreds of people. His wheels were on tarmac over what had been Bean Street.

Instead he started up his engine and, the Devil costume on the front seat beside him, drove back to the police station and to the murder room.

Once inside he unrolled the costume, and once again ran his fingers expertly over the glove ends to the arms. The tips of the fabric gloves were decorated by talons carefully made by props, but he ignored those. His sensitive finger ends were exploring the smooth dark red fabric between the base of the thumb and the first knuckle area of the first finger, of the right-hand glove. Even in the strong unwavering light of his own work room there was nothing to see, but fingertips are incredibly sensitive, and his had sensed a thickening and stiffening of the fabric in one tiny area.

The station was quiet; it was by now late at night. Most of his own team had gone home.

'It will have to wait until morning,' thought Bob. 'No, dammit. I'm not willing to wait.'

To a determined police officer there are places where, with a little coaxing, even at midnight someone will look under a microscope at a little scrap of fabric – half an inch by one eighth – where something is stiff which ought to be soft.

'Blood,' said the pathologist, who had just got home from a party when the phone rang, and who had welcomed a little more excitement before bed. They were in his laboratory at the hospital.

'Whose blood?'

'Can't tell you that. Only the blood group. Hang on … a rare group,' he said at last. 'Very unusual indeed. A2B Rhesus Negative NN.'

Bob had not realized until then that he was holding his breath.

He clenched his hand round an imaginary dagger, and struck out in front of him, then in dumb show indicated the area of his hand between the base of the thumb and the first joint of the index finger.

'Yes.'

'Not much doubt of it?'

'I should say none. This is a blood group for only one in fifty thousand people, and it is Bruce Exelby's blood group.'

12

When I was sick and sorriest,
You came not nigh, for I was poor.
The Mercers' Play

It was not until the plays were in their third
and most triumphant week that, on waking
at two in the morning, Thomas Churchyard
remembered the small but significant point
which had struck him as incongruous as he
stood looking down from the steps of
Heaven on to the alert, stirring cast of the
mystery plays waiting among the graves of St
Olave's.

He had been dreaming about the scene.
His first thought on waking was that he
really mustn't let the affair get on top of him.
Dreaming about it was just ridiculous. The
vision was still in his mind, more real than
the bedside lamp, the darkness of the
summer night outside the curtains, the book
which lay ready for wakefulness on his
bedside table.

Once he had remembered, the solution
was obvious, but it took him a while to work
it out. And then sorrow washed over him in
a great wave. He could see How. He could

see Who. He could not see Why.

The obvious thing to do at two in the morning was to go back to sleep, and first thing in the morning to walk next door and tell Bob Southwell all about it. And that was precisely what he felt he could not do.

Sleep, of course, turned out to be impossible. All that happened when he lay down and drew the light covers up to his chin was that the thing made itself more and more clear to him as it revolved round and round unceasingly in his head.

As for going to Bob Southwell ... that was what he ought to do. Ought, perhaps, to ring him now, waking him from whatever slumbers he was having, with an apparently unsolvable murder on his hands and extra staff no longer at his disposal. That was what he had told Sydney Absolom to do, go to the police. That was what Sydney Absolom had never had time to do. Before he got there he had tipped out of a window ... or been pushed ... that suddenly looked even more likely... 'And I can't go either,' thought Tom.

'Even if I put myself in danger by not picking up the phone now, this minute, and ringing Bob?

'Even if...

'Why? That's what I can't understand.

'If I go to Bob Southwell and tell him what I now believe I put another human being on the spot without giving them any opportunity to consider; perhaps to repent, perhaps to give themselves up to the police because they realize that what they've done is wrong, morally wrong, that they have imperilled their mortal soul by taking the life of another – perhaps two other – human beings.

'If I go to Bob Southwell I am playing God with someone else's life.

'Am I entitled to do that, to take that power, as if they were a rag doll with no self-determination? Who am I, to go to Bob and point the finger, to say, this person is guilty, arrest them, try them for murder?

'Have I no loyalty towards this person? Yes, I have.

'What happens if I tell them themselves, what I suspect? Discuss it with them? Try to make them see that their only course is to go to the police themselves ... or to take their own life ... would they do that? Would that not compound the sin, rather than cleanse it? Would that be any better than a long prison sentence or a lifetime in a mental institution?

'Confession is good for the soul,' thought Thomas.

He was sometimes emotional and religious in the night like this. During the day he was a mightily efficient engineer with a degree in electronics and a section of an important department to run. But in the still watches of the night primeval Thomas emerged, doubting, fearful, reliant on the ideas first instilled in him at his mother's knee, influenced by the thoughts and principles of the medieval period he loved so much. He could think now only in large, grand ideas, of responsibility and restitution, of immortal souls, of sin and death.

He lay there and struggled with the inside of his brain as the rest of the summer night passed away and the early dawn came, and still returned to the one dominating thought; I cannot play God with another's life.

The Thomas who at last thought it was late enough to get up and begin the day was a more straightforward man. This was a Thomas who did not beat about the bush, and if he had a task to do went ahead and did it.

He did go to see Bob Southwell, as soon as he thought it reasonable. He went to the back door and Linda opened it. He could see through the utility room and into the kitchen where the children were eating boiled eggs.

'Oh, I'm sorry, Tom,' said Linda. 'Bob's already left. He's living and sleeping this case at the moment. If he isn't down there he's sitting thinking about it. He couldn't settle this morning. Some new idea seems to have hit him late last night – he wasn't in until the early hours – so he's gone down to fiddle with that computer.'

'I think I know who did it. I'll go to see him,' said Tom. He was intending to, of course. But he could not get away from the idea that to do so was unfairly to influence another's destiny. Who was Thomas Churchyard to give a person up to justice? What right had he to point the finger? And was he sure? He had gone to see Bob and Bob was not there. Was this chance, or an omen? A pointer? An augury? Was this a signpost to what he ought to do?

He looked vague and withdrawn as he nodded at Linda and walked away. She closed the door again faintly puzzled and a little worried.

It was a lovely June morning and although heat was promised for later, at present it was warm enough to be pleasant and not too hot. Thomas decided to walk. Twenty minutes or so to think about what he was doing would not be a bad thing.

He walked from Clifton along Bootham. He turned left into Gillygate – called after St Giles – and passed its varied buildings. It was recovering from planning blights, and all the little interesting projects which had found a cheap home there would gradually give way, he supposed, to the rampant materialism and money-making bustle of the other shopping streets.

At present it was still an interesting place, narrow-pavemented, leading to a large car park where coaches disembarked their passengers who then walked in long bunches into the tourist areas of the city. Thomas had to step off the kerb, risking his life under the wheels of the fuming lorries, or squeeze himself into doorways three separate times to avoid such phalanxes of determined tourists.

Portland Street is a short road leading to the playing fields of Bootham School. Having trees and grass at the end of the cul-de-sac and a few small trees and shrubs in the minute front gardens saves it from being totally arid. On that June morning parked cars and motorbikes, the sound of a transistor, raucous purple paint on one tall flat-fronted house and posters in the window of another gave the place a slightly rakish modern air, superimposed on its basically Edwardian style.

Tom knocked on a door and after a few seconds it was answered by Velvet Smith, neatly and tidily dressed as always, and nondescript as ever. She looked surprised to see him.

'There was something I wanted to ask you about,' he said awkwardly.

'Well, come in, Thomas. Is it too early for coffee?'

Her rather blank dark eyes did not show surprise, although he had never been to her house before, and although it was barely nine o'clock in the morning. 'Is something wrong about the plays?'

'No, it's not that... A coffee would be welcome.'

'Come in.'

He stood in the entrance hall. A flight of steps carpeted in a vigorously patterned Axminster rose straight in front of him. To the right were two doors, obviously to front and back rooms. A passage running alongside the stairs led to the kitchen door. The floor of the entrance and passage was of encaustic tiles in an elaborate pattern. The woodwork was all massive and moulded, grained and varnished dark brown.

Tom was a little taken aback. Although some things were modern, the feel of the house was of a previous generation. It had a strong presence; it was borne in upon him that it was like a lodging house; it had that impersonal, predatory feel.

Velvet, after some apparent hesitation about which room to use, led him into the dining room, at the back. Sure enough, there were three tables – two of them gatelegs, folded and standing against the wall – and about a dozen chairs. On the walls were photographs of actors and actresses, many of them signed.

She watched him as his glance swept the room, and smiled sardonically.

'I didn't realize,' he said.

'You didn't realize?'

'Presumably,' said Tom with an effort,

'these are people you knew?'

'Yes. My parents ran a lodging house, mainly for theatricals. This area was noted for it. Have you been in York so long and didn't know that? The whole cast of a visiting company could be accommodated along here somewhere, and a good few of the regular repertory company as well.'

'It must have been interesting.'

'It was darned hard work. Theatrical landladies are often joked about. It wasn't much of a joke being one. Interesting, yes, compared to other kinds of lodging houses. But with lots of disadvantages.'

Tom felt acutely disinclined for coffee, but he had accepted the offer, and so he sat down when Velvet indicated a chair. The window looked on to a narrow back yard, which had been made brighter by containers planted with flowers. He thought he could smell old odours of boiled cabbage, soot, and furniture polish.

Velvet brought a tray with two cups. She poured hot milk and coffee from the matching jugs.

Tom had been thinking a good many things. Such as: perhaps a longing for the stage had imbued Mrs Smith, and made her choose theatrical lodgers; such as: he had never noticed before the practised competence with which Velvet served drinks. Most women he knew served drinks competently so he had not realized that she had a different air altogether when doing it – the air of someone who has done such things in a service capacity; such as: her involvement with acting and the stage had continued with MRS and with the mystery plays. Tom did not know how to approach the subject which had brought him.

'Did you know Bruce Exelby when he was a young actor, then?' he said at last.

She seemed as if she was never going to answer. A strange expression crossed the face he thought he knew well. 'Yes, I did know him,' she said at last.

He sipped his coffee and looked at her. Velvet was plain; there was no getting away from it. She was also inexpressive. Her thoughts did not show themselves on her face. It was a pale, pudgy face, neither fat nor thin, but lacking in tone. Her dull darkish hair was short and close to her head. Her eyes were dark, about the same rather nondescript colour as her hair. Her nose was so ordinary that it defied him to find any other adjective to describe it.

'I never remember you talking to him on the set, Velvet,' he said at last, trying to keep his voice normal. 'I don't remember that at all.'

'He never showed me a flicker of recognition.'

'Did he ever lodge with you?'

'Oh yes. All the time. It was a second home to him. He lived with us all the time he was in York – two years.'

'He must have forgotten.' Tom did not like to say 'Perhaps you've changed,' but she seemed to pick up his thought.

'Oh! I was always unobtrusive and insignificant.'

'I wouldn't say that, Velvet.'

'You would, because I am. I'm not insulted. Believe me, it can be very useful.'

Useful, in doing things without being noticed. Tom sipped again at his coffee. It was hot. Even in his elevated and agonized state he appreciated good coffee. And hers had come out of the same jug, and she had drunk quite a lot of it.

'Being small can be useful too, I expect,' he said. 'Small enough to wear a costume made for a large child.'

She looked at him steadily.

'I wonder what you are getting at, Tom. I wonder why you came here.'

'I have guessed something about the murder.'

'Why didn't you go straight to the police with your guesses? Why come to me?'

'It may sound silly. Because if I had accused – a certain somebody – I would have been manipulating another person's life without their being aware of it. If I go to the police it will be with your knowledge.'

'*My* knowledge?...' She sat very straight, and looked intently at him. 'And what will you tell them, Tom?'

Tom felt very cold. This was what he had come to do, yet now he felt afraid – not afraid of Velvet, but afraid of making himself look a fool. Such a basic, human fear. How many good and right actions have not been carried out because someone was afraid of looking a fool? Afraid that his night-time deductions were wrong. Afraid of coming out with the accusation, 'You killed.'

'I will tell them,' he said at last, 'that I believe that late on the night of the last dress rehearsal, while Sally Vause came round to see a bit of the production, or maybe just to chat to friends, as she did most evenings, you put on the costume of the little Devil who'd been thrown out of the production for that bit of criminal stupidity with the willow branch – that you ran along in the growing darkness to the Museum Gardens – that you went in under the stage and found Exelby for a moment alone – that you stabbed him – that after stabbing him you ran and joined the other Devils in the smoke and flames of Hell's Mouth – and when they were sent away after Exelby died, you ran ahead of them – probably even on that night they stopped to make wailing noises to scare the Angels, or just to speak to them, to tell them what had happened – and that you had taken off the costume by the time they and Sally Vause returned to St Olave's parish room.'

Velvet was very still. It seemed as if inwardly she was concentrating all her forces into a still centre. Her voice, when it came, was still, stone still, and deadly as that of a snake.

'All very clever,' she said. 'And what led you to this brilliant conclusion?'

'I saw you,' said Tom miserably. She became even tenser and more still. 'I saw you run from near the Etty monument, across the grass, and round the end of the wall to join the other Devils.'

'Where were you?'

'On the scaffolding.'

'And you saw a Devil run across and thought it was me dressed as a devil? What made you think that? For the rest is all taradiddle and supposition, Tom.'

'A woman doesn't run like a boy,' said Tom miserably. 'Her hips rotate more, even if she is small and slim. It was not a boy's run. It was the run of a woman. It was your run, Velvet. I haven't seen you run but the more I think of it the more convinced I am.'

'So you think I am a murderess.'

'I don't want to think that. You and I are friends, as well as colleagues in MRS... I thought all the members of MRS were my friends. But ... the Etty monument is only a few yards from the place under the stage where Exelby was stabbed. The time was right. You had every opportunity for doing what I have described – you are in charge of the costumes when Sally is not there. No one can be recognized once they have those frightful devil costumes and masks on.'

'Don't give me any friendship stuff, Thomas. You're on the point of – as you think – shopping me to the police with this story. I can't understand why you didn't do just that, instead of coming to me first. I might have a stiletto handy. You've never noticed me in MRS, so don't pretend you have. I was just useful, as I have been all my life.'

'Very useful,' responded Tom, in hearty but assumed approbation.

'Why did you come here accusing me?'

'I thought you could only have done it out of some sort of misery. It didn't seem understandable. I wanted to give you the chance to go to the police yourself. It would be better.'

'Oh yes,' her eyes seemed to bore straight through him. 'Oh yes. I did it,' said Velvet slowly. 'You have guessed correctly, dear Thomas. I did it.'

He could hardly speak. At last: 'But why?'

'For revenge. One will do a great deal for revenge.'

'What harm had Exelby done you?'

'Oh, that!' Her eyelids fell over those normally inexpressive dark eyes. 'It seems long ago now. It was a burning grievance for so many years, urgent. And now the wrong is avenged it is receding. I could start a new life now. I could start to really live for the first time. But for you and your friendly neighbourhood policeman, that Southwell, Thomas. But for you.'

'Was it you he wronged?' Tom felt odd using such a Victorian-sounding phrase. He was thinking the conventional thing – that Bruce had made her fall in love with him and then jilted her; perhaps there had even been a child.

'Oh no!' Her lids went up and she looked at him intently now. 'I was as insignificant to him as I am to you. He didn't trifle with my affections, if that's what you're thinking. Oh no.'

Tom just sat and looked at her. He had never envisaged any scene like this. She was playing with the spoon in her coffee cup, turning it over and over with a small metallic irritating sound.

'Oh no, I don't matter.'

'Of course you matter!...' Tom heard himself again being over-hearty.

'He ruined my parents' lives, Tom. It is as simple as that. I revenged them. It is over now.'

'Tell me?'

'All big talk, he was, about the productions he was going to do which would make such a lot of profit. He carried my mother away on a tide of talk, and persuaded my father to give him a large loan. Then he went off and got this great production off the ground, inspired, produced and directed by himself.'

'I remember he made his name with the musical, *Pink Nocturne*. It did tremendously well.'

'It was a great success. Not so great on the balance sheet, because the production costs were so colossal. It broke even, made a small profit. It was Bruce Exelby's springboard into the big time, and he never looked back.'

'And your father got his loan back? With interest I hope.'

'My father got nothing. Bruce had promised us the earth – we were to be at the first night of the show – he would let us have the money back within six months – he would never forget our kindness – we would always be his closest friends and our home his second home. When at last my father asked for the money – he didn't ask for a long time – Bruce told him that he had understood the money to be a gift, not a loan. He never returned a penny.'

'But couldn't your father...'

'Have sued him? There was nothing in writing. That money was every penny he had, Tom. All his savings after a lifetime working for the railway. He had been planning to retire the next year. His health was poor and he was tired. It's no picnic working full time

301

and then in the evening helping your wife to run a boarding house.'

'Legal action?'

'He took legal advice and there was nothing he could do. He'd even raised a mortgage on this house to help Bruce. He'd been taken for everything he'd got by a con man, who was now leading the glittering life. Bruce just kept on repeating that it had been a gift, and it was his word against my father's.'

'What happened?'

'Well, I still live here you see, so you know we pulled through – I did, at least. Instead of retiring my father worked until the week he died. I had to watch him getting greyer and greyer, thinner and thinner. I left school at fifteen and worked, daytime, evenings, weekends. Mother ran this place on a shoestring. That didn't make her the most popular landlady in the street. We scrimped, ourselves. We didn't know what it was to have new clothes or go on holiday. Day in, day out we struggled to keep our heads above water. Week by week we counted every penny. Dad and I walked to work. Mother gave up using the laundry and did all the washing herself at home. We sold everything we could from the house – everything the guests didn't see went.'

'Why didn't you ask him for the money back?'

'Oh, we did. Many and many a time, until

we got a solicitor's letter threatening action if we didn't stop bothering the great director. He didn't know us, didn't want to know us, didn't know what we were talking about, owed us nothing. I remember the words. They are burned into my brain as they were into my father's. I took Bruce Exelby's life to avenge my father. As I drove the knife home, I said, "That's for my father."'

'How could you, Velvet?'

'Quite easily, believe me. It corrodes you inside, a long hatred. I felt nothing but satisfaction as I used his own knife on him.'

'His own knife?'

'Yes. He gave it to us as a keepsake after the York production of Hamlet. It has hung for many years on the wall of my bedroom. I have looked at it every night before going to sleep and every morning on waking. It was about the only thing we didn't sell. I would never have sold it. It was a focus for my hatred. Now it has gone, all there is is a mark on the wallpaper, a mark the shape of the dagger.'

Thomas suddenly realized he was still holding the cup from which he had drunk coffee. His fingers had clenched so tightly round the fragile handle that when he settled the cup carefully into the depression on the saucer, and relaxed his hold, the handle fell in pieces.

He had in the last few minutes felt profoundly sorry for her and her family, and that he too might have longed to take revenge. Then his feelings changed. Theatrical landladies were not soft touches as a rule. Surely her father should have had more sense than to make an unsecured loan. Had they brought on this loss themselves, by coming forward like lambs eager to be fleeced? Surely the lawyers could have done something – surely Exelby could have been shamed into paying the debt...

'I can't stay here, Velvet. I must get out into the air.'

'You're not going, Thomas. You came here and brought this up, you can't just go like that. Sit still and listen. The past counts, you see, Thomas,' she said. 'You've always got your eyes fixed either on the present with your work or on the medieval past. You forget that there are other pasts, nearer than the Middle Ages. They matter too. You've come to live in York and think it very pretty and imagine yourself back in time. There's a lot of living you ignore by doing that.'

He stood up. Somehow it did not occur to him at that moment that he himself was in any personal danger. He looked down at her.

'Didn't you realize that revenge is in other hands than yours? "Vengeance is mine, said the Lord."'

'Revenge was mine and it was sweet. Sit

down, Thomas. Here's another cup. We'll both drink some more coffee. We have things to talk about.'

Thomas realized that he was shaking. It must be useless arguing with a self-confessed murderess. But he had to try to make her see, and to gain time to think. His voice became forceful.

'I can't seem to bring it home to you, Velvet. The really terrible thing is "looking at evil and calling it good, looking at good and calling it evil". You committed an evil act – how else can one describe murder? – and you call it good. It was not good. You were not right to take vengeance. If what Exelby did was terrible, what you did was more terrible – to yourself.'

'It was the greatest satisfaction of my life. I thrust in his own knife, up to the hilt. I avenged.'

'At what cost?'

'I don't care what cost.'

'At what cost to yourself? All these years you have allowed this hatred and desire for revenge to eat you away inside. You have been a walking whited sepulchre.'

She looked at him and laughed in a way that chilled his blood.

'You are getting biblical with a vengeance, Tom. It's all this God business. All right, I'm eaten away inside. That man ruined two people I loved. I'm not capable of love any

305

more, only of hate. You think because I was in your silly little society that I am a mate, a pal, a friend did you say? Not me. I joined because Exelby was going to direct the mystery plays, and I knew that Sally Vause would almost certainly be in charge of costume, and it struck me as a useful society to be in to get to the position to do what I did. Sorry, Tom. You are an altruist, aren't you? What a sucker!'

'Right from the start…?'

'Yes. I joined MRS the week the director's appointment was announced, last year.'

'The opportunity might not have occurred.'

'Opportunities are made. That was my last night with the real chance of action – he was going away the next day after the first performance, and I did not dare leave it to the last. I would have preferred it to be on the first night of the production, with all the audience in front.'

'That would have ruined the production completely… Could you work among everyone for months – and feel nothing of the comradeship, the community feeling?'

She snapped her fingers. 'That for your community feeling. There's only one way to get what you want in life and that's to take the matter into your own hands and do it yourself. Bruce Exelby taught me a good deal. He taught me to hate and to be strong. And to seize opportunities, and improvise.

And if you're thinking of Sydney Absolom, yes ... his death was not an accident. I did it to him too, because he told you he had found out who killed Exelby and was going to tell the police. I was coming into the room looking for a water carafe and overheard him talking, so I stood behind the door and waited. You left without noticing me, Tom. I told you that it is useful, being insignificant. That was an impulse, I'm afraid. Although I was really rather pleased with my improvisation and its success. Stupid Syd! Why did he have to stick his nose in?'

'Because he was being accused.'

'Rubbish! He wouldn't have harmed a fly. Anyone with half an eye could see that. Anyway – he's just between you and me. The coroner's verdict on him was accidental death. If an old man leans out of a high window on a scorching day he's asking for a dizzy spell.'

'You're not even sorry?'

'Yes, I am. I'm sorry about Sydney. I liked him and up till then he'd never done me any harm.'

Thomas was feeling very sick. The last thing he wanted was Velvet's coffee yet he seemed to have no alternative but to drink more. She had replaced the broken cup and was lifting the two jugs. Twin streams came down into first her own cup and then his. He realized that it was going to be difficult

307

to get away.

'I want you to make your mind up what to do,' he said. 'Are you going to tell the police yourself?'

'No fear.'

'I will give you twenty-four hours to make up your mind on a course of action.'

'No need. My course of action has been determined by you this morning. I can't stay here now. I shall pack and go abroad before the police can stop me.'

'I can't let you do that, Velvet,' he said gravely.

'And how are you going to stop me?'

'By force if necessary. But I'd rather it was with an appeal to your conscience. Tell a jury what you've told me and you should get off lightly. Not that I'm condoning anything – that's just the way it will probably be.'

'I have no conscience, Tom. If you are going to stand in the way you will have to be number three.'

Poison was having an interview with his agent and road manager. They had both come north to take him over when the last night of the plays released him.

'I gotta have a bit of time off,' he told them. 'No way am I going on tour again just yet.'

'Just some recording sessions, boyo,' said the agent. 'That's all you got lined up for the next month. Then we start thinking about a tour of America – the big one. Unless of course you want to stay in this acting lark. There's an offer in from the RSC of a straight part if you want it, a lead, starring role.'

'I dunno.'

'Doesn't pay like singing does,' put in the road manager.

'Too right, but it's up to you, boyo.'

'Look, I wanna give my next tour a new slant. I've got ideas for some new songs.'

'Sounds good.'

'I wanna work up some ideas on the theme of reconciliation.'

'Of what, boyo?'

'Reconciliation, and the redeeming power of love.'

'You going all religious, mate? Cliff Richard does all right with that. Might work out.'

'Dammit, I'm not!'

'Calm down.'

Poison threw himself on to the checked counterpane of the caravan bed, and gazed at the ceiling.

'Just wait, wilya?' he said. 'Wait until I've had time to get my ideas into shape. I need a lot of hours in the studio with a session man on drums, maybe. There's music running through my head, words. I've gotta have time to work them out. Then we'll give them a try on the next tour.'

'And if they're a frost?'

'Then too bad. They would have to go.'

'Well... OK, if you realize that...'

'I realize that.'

'And what do I say to the RSC?'

'Tell them not now. One day I might want to act again, but not right now.'

'OK.'

'Now beat it, you two. Go feed the ducks. I've got things to do. I want to see a mate of mine.'

Bob Southwell had arrived at the end of a long piece of patient reasoning and deduction. He was sure he had the person, the opportunity, and the method by which that opportunity had been utilized, though motive was still obscure. He got up from the computer desk with a long-drawn-out sigh of tired satisfaction. The girl computer operator appeared in the doorway with a cup of coffee.

'Nine twenty-five, sir,' she said. 'You aren't supposed to look at that thing for more than two hours without a break. Bad for the eyes. Please move away from the machine while you drink this, it ruins them if you spill coffee on them. Accidentally, of course,' she added hastily.

'I haven't been using it solidly.' Southwell sounded quite mild.

'No, sir. If you'll excuse me saying so,

310

you've been sitting gazing at the screen while you were thinking more than you've been using it.'

'I've hardly used it at all. The work's been going on in my mind.'

'It would still fit in better with police regulations for computer users if you came over here and drank this coffee, sir.'

She thought that Bob Southwell was like a carving knife, thin, bright, keen, and liable to cut, to be treated with respect. He came over to the side desk quite amiably and drank the coffee. Before he had finished it, there was a knock at the door and a constable came in.

'Someone asking urgently for you, sir.'

'Who is it?'

'Mr Poison Peters.'

Bob looked irritated. At this juncture, he could do without the pop star, whom he had never liked anyway.

'He's very insistent that it's urgent. Seems to think someone's in danger.'

'Let him in.'

'Yes?' he said shortly.

'D'ya know where Tom Churchyard is?' asked Poison, in a breath.

'At home still at this time, I should think.'

'Well he isn't. And before he left he went to your house and asked for you, said he'd made deductions and wanted to tell you who done it. Isn't that what that other bloke

311

said – the one that fell out of the window? That he knew who it was and was going to tell the fuzz?'

'That's right,' said Bob, putting down the empty coffee cup and rising to his feet. 'If Tom's come to the same conclusion as me and decided to confront her with it instead of coming to me...'

'That's exactly what I've been thinking. It must be a woman. A woman who's been brooding on some injury for a long time, and gone bitter and twisted inside. And Tom would feel all chivalrous, and not want to shop her to the fuzz.'

Bob regarded Poison in amazement. He gave him credit for unexpected powers of logical thought. 'And there aren't many women who had the opportunity. What time did he go to my house?'

Policeman and pop star looked at one another.

'About twenty to nine. D'yar know where she lives?'

'Yes. Come on.' Not for a second did Bob think of standing on protocol and making Poison stay behind.

On his rapid stride through the police station Bob collected two of his staff and outside they embarked in two cars, Bob and Poison in the first and the two detectives in the other.

They put the sirens on and screamed

through the streets. Within the cars no one spoke. They turned up Portland Street and drew up with a protest of brakes.

'He's a big bloke,' Poison said as they jumped out, 'and she's small.'

'Doesn't follow that he'd win, if she staged a physical attack,' retorted Bob. 'Find your way round the back,' he said to the two detectives, and directed them with a gesture. Ringing the doorbell madly he waited – one second – two seconds – three seconds–

He tried the handle at the same time. The door was held by a small Yale lock. Poison expected to see him put his shoulder to the door like they do in films. Instead Bob moved over to the sash window in the front bay. It was open just a crack at the bottom. With a strong clasp-knife blade he levered it up. As soon as the window was six inches above the sill he put his leg into the room, and then shoved the window sharply upward.

'No time to stand on ceremony,' he said. Poison followed. They burst hastily but fairly quietly into the front hallway – then into the dining room, for the open door of the kitchen showed that to be empty – and without a word Southwell, grabbing her from the back, pinioned Velvet Smith's arms behind her.

Thomas Churchyard was standing there as if frozen.

The two detectives had managed to get in

through the back yard and the unlocked back door. Holding her carefully as though she might sting, Bob handed Velvet Smith over to them.

'I arrest you, Velvet Smith, for the murder of Bruce Exelby and suspected murder of Sydney Absolom... Take her down to the station, you two. Charge her. Watch her like a hawk.'

Velvet's face was that of a fury. 'You said you hadn't told them,' she hissed at Thomas. 'You said no one knew where you were.'

'I didn't tell them.'

'We can sometimes work things out for ourselves, Miss Smith,' said Bob sarcastically.

Velvet was taken out of the room. He turned to Thomas. 'What the hell do you think you're doing?'

Tom drew himself up, and looked rueful.

Poison came forward.

'If it hadn't been for your friend here you'd have been a goner, if she'd had her way,' Bob said. 'If he hadn't come to me when he did I might have been another hour or two – might even have decided to wait for the end of the mystery play production – after all it's nearly over. Has she hurt you in any way?' Bob seemed to realize that he was not being very sympathetic.

'Physically, you mean? No. What could she

314

have done to me?' asked Thomas, still rigid with the shock of the recent conversation. 'I'm twice her size.'

'So what?' Bob was reminded painfully of his little daughter's unintentioned physical victory over his athletic son. 'I wouldn't put it past her to hurt you. You seem to forget what she's already done. If she's studied self-defence,' Bob added sharply, 'a hard kick on your kneecap would have had you writhing on the floor. Then she could have done a good bit of damage with ammonia which she probably has in the kitchen, or a kettle of hot water, or anything else which was handy.'

'Then she'd have finished up with a big corpse to dispose of, which would not have been very sensible of her. No. She hadn't got started on the kneecaps. She's hurt me enough other ways. I didn't know anyone could look so evil, or that anyone close to me was so treacherous. I can't get over it, the horror of the way she is.'

'There's no doubt no rational woman would have attacked you. I wouldn't care to tackle you myself. But she's not rational any more, Tom.'

'Come on,' Poison looked at Thomas keenly. 'Come and have a cup of tea.'

'I think I've drunk enough for one morning.' Thomas produced a nervous laugh.

'Well come and have something. A

Marmite sandwich.'

'I'll be glad to get out of this place. What an atmosphere! Thick with hatred.'

'I want you at the station for a statement, but have your sandwich first and a natter if you want.'

'No, I'll come and get it over with.'

'I'll come with you,' said Poison.

Poison settled into the back of the car as if police cars were his favourite mode of transport. Together he and Tom went into an interview room, and for a minute they were alone.

'Look Tom, this isn't the time or the place,' said Poison, 'but I'd like you to use my real name. It's John. There aren't many people I ask to do that.'

He looked very young and very serious.

Thomas smiled at him. 'You're a pal, John,' he said and they shook hands formally.

Bob Southwell came into the room. 'We'll take your statements now.'

'How is Velvet? I feel responsible for all this. She is our treasurer in MRS.'

'Your responsibility is over now if you ever had any. Detecting, and taking care of a criminal, is part of my profession, Tom. It seems to have been your accidental vocation, but that's over. Now, the statement...'

There was a crowd at York station, but there were no banners. Tom, Clare the Virgin

316

Mary, Lucifer, and a few others, were at the front and a miscellaneous collection of York citizens at the back. The train was due to leave for London in five minutes.

A long car drew up, and Poison got out, taking care not to damage the spikes of his pale hair. The crowd broke into a cheer, one fan screamed and sobbed, and he smiled at them out of a pale face with rouged lips, batted his long mascara-ed eyelashes over the vivid golden brown eyes, and spread his arms wide as if to embrace them all, thin bony hands combing the air. The mid-summer sun struck lightning out of his silver jacket and lost its beams in the blackness of his soft shirt with the embroidered five-pointed star across the breast. A solitary cameraman stepped forward and flashed a light bulb. The reporter from the *Yorkshire Post* asked a last question.

'Yeah,' said Poison. 'I love your beautiful city, yeah.'

This Large Print Book, for people
who cannot read normal print,
is published under the auspices of

THE ULVERSCROFT FOUNDATION

The publishers hope that this book has given you enjoyable reading. Large Print Books are especially designed to be as easy to see and hold as possible. If you wish a complete list of our books please ask at your local library or write directly to:

Dales Large Print Books
Magna House, Long Preston,
Skipton, North Yorkshire.
BD23 4ND